Joan Barfoot is an internationally acclaimed novelist. Her novel, *Gaining Ground* (The Women's Press, 1980), won the Books in Canada award as the best first novel of the year when it was published under the title *Abra*. Her other novels are *Duet for Three* (The Women's Press, 1986) and *Family News* (The Women's Press, 1990), both Feminist Book Fortnight Selected Twenty Titles; *Plain Jane* (The Women's Press, 1992); *Charlotte and Claudia Keeping in Touch* (The Women's Press, 1994); *Some Things About Flying* (The Women's Press, 1997); and *Getting Over Edgar* (The Women's Press, 1999). Joan Barfoot lives in London, Ontario.

Also by Joan Barfoot from The Women's Press:

Gaining Ground (1980)
Duet for Three (1986)
Family News (1990)
Plain Jane (1992)
Charlotte and Claudia Keeping in Touch (1994)
Some Things About Flying (1997)
Getting Over Edgar (1999)

joan barfoot
dancing in the dark

Published in Great Britain by The Women's Press Ltd, 1982
A member of the Namara Group
34 Great Sutton Street, London EC1V 0LQ
www.the-womens-press.com

Reprinted 1984, 1992, 2000

First published in Canada by Macmillan of Canada, 1982
A Division of Gage Publishing Ltd

British Library Cataloguing-in-Publication Data

Barfoot, Joan
Dancing in the dark.
I. Title
813í.54[F] PR9199.3.B3715

ISBN 0 7043 4674 5

Printed and bound in Great Britain by Cox & Wyman,
Reading, Berkshire

1

I BIND MY WOUNDS WITH PAPER; with this blue notebook, a garish shade not eggshell nor sky nor water, but a colour too blunt and striking. There are spaces on the cover labelled, in black print, Name _____; and below that, Subject _____. The date is August 17. I asked the nurse.

In tiny print in the bottom left-hand corner it says the book is printed with recycled paper. And that, I think, is good. I have always approved of that sort of thing, when I have thought about it.

Inside, the notebook is lined thinly with grey, a pink stripe marking a margin at the side of each page, three holes cut into each margin, round and precise, not at all like the holes, irregular and unspaced, made by a knife in a body. There is a comforting neatness about this book, so one feels compelled either to leave it blank or to write in it carefully, perfectly, and with a certain pain in the perfection.

I appreciate things that are careful, complete, and perfect. This day, for instance. I am fortunate to have a place beside the big window, so that I can look out without obstruction.

Here, of course, there is an unchanging temperature, an untouchability in the atmosphere. So I cannot tell if outside it is uncomfortably hot, but I think not; I think it is a day in which heat soaks the body like a liniment and heals.

Yesterday it rained. But since I am safe inside here, that too was fine, and I watched the greyness falling mist-like. The result of the rain is that in today's sunshine there is an extra greenness, an almost-too-shrill brightness. It is all quite clearly defined; there are perceptible boundaries between the green of the grass and the tree-trunk-grey and the deep green leaves, no blending to confuse.

On such a day the mind should also be distinct.

It is the details with which I may occupy myself, nothing larger than this room, this body. I shall attempt neatness and keep removed from passion.

The bed is narrow, sheeted with white, coarse. The bed I used to have was wide, the sheets were blue and in the winter covered by the deep down quilt made far back in my mother's family, in aging rags of blue, soft yellow, checkered red and white. That bed did not have buttons to be pushed that raise shiny steel bars at the sides, an extra bulk that spoils the simplicity of the lines. And it was softer too, while this one is hard and tightly wrapped.

There are two such beds in this room. One is mine, and I am careful to stay in it, or near it, never stray too far, for although it may be strange and ugly, it is also mine.

I can reach out and touch it from where I sit in the easy chair, the blue-and-purple-patterned chair that fills the space between the narrow bed and the wide, heavy-glass window. I sit with my legs crossed at the ankles, back pressed firmly against the chair, blue notebook opened squarely on my lap, my knees touching the base of the window ledge while still in my line of vision on the other side is the glimpse of unwrinkled sheet-whiteness. Three feet, perhaps, between bed and window.

It is precisely the right amount of space. This much I can manage, most days.

At the foot of my bed, a narrow pathway distant, is a dresser, a double one that extends the width of my bed and beyond into the other half of the room, a double dresser with mirror, drawers of underwear shared, split into mine and other. Over the centre of my half is a cheap framed landscape, autumn trees with unreal red and gold leaves, a too-blue stream running past steel-grey rocks. Not the sort of painting I would choose, and yet it is oddly right for this room.

Overhead there is a fluorescent light, switched on at dusk and on dull days. Attached to the headboard of the bed is a reading lamp, which must not be used after a certain hour. When it gets dark, cream-coloured curtains are drawn across the windows and there is no more to see.

It is a puzzling half-room, clumsily warm, but not personal. Some things I like about it though: that it is arranged in straight lines; that is is always in order; that I am responsible for none of it.

The days are slow, events are rare. No one makes me move. The farthest I go from my narrow half-room is to the dining area three times a day; the second farthest when I again pass the other bed, the other half of the double dresser, the second and near-identical landscape on the wall, the closet, to go to the washroom. There are two of us in this room, with a washroom connecting with two others in the next room. To be sure of privacy in the bathroom, it is necessary to lock two doors: the one from Room 201, which is mine, and the one from Room 203, which is next door. Sometimes when I sit on the toilet and do not care to move, for it is white and bright in there, a door handle may move and there may be a muffled remark, but I pay no attention. To move, even if I wanted to, is an effort of will, and I am somewhat short of will these days.

And too, consumed as I am by the trivialities of my own existence, a piece of lint on my housecoat, the glint of a straight pin on the carpet by my chair — and how would such a thing get there if not through me, and I have no use for straight pins, a puzzle to occupy some moments — how should I then have attention for those others? I am careful not to see them. I want to know nothing about them. I take special care in my own half-room never to glance beyond my bed, never to acknowledge the mutters and rustlings from the other bed, never to meet eyes. If it were possible, I would roll my eyes inward and stare only at myself.

When I am to be dressed, someone does it for me. They get me up and seat me; sometimes even brush my teeth. I would have my food, too, spooned into me except that that would make a contact, it would be difficult to avoid the eyes and too much trouble, and so I feed myself. I wait, though, until the meat has been cut for me. Otherwise I would have to take it in my hands to gnaw, for I cannot imagine myself carving it up.

On the good days, it can be restful. On the bad days, it does not matter how still I try to be: the heartbeat is fierce, the sweat pours, the trembling begins. I don't quite know where it comes from, but I can always feel it waiting. Which is why I have to consider so carefully the lint on the housecoat, the pin in the carpet, why the back must be straight and the ankles crossed just so, why this notebook must be set squarely on the lap and the handwriting school-taught and correct. I do not permit erasures, no blots or irregularities are allowed.

I am afraid. I am afraid of changes and things that are not precise. I make vast efforts at perfection, because I fear what may come of flaws. Disaster waits for mistakes. I want everything to be right. There are places for all things, and proper ways of thinking about them. There must be order in salvation. But it's so hard; it is not easy to maintain precision and perfection. It is a constant labour, and it is necessary always to be on guard. The long fall, a great chasm, waits for a tiny slip.

2

I DON'T SEE HIM WHOLE, only bits and pieces. And of those bits and pieces, his hands most clearly. I cannot imagine having married a different shape of hands. Never the short, squat, broad, fur-knuckled kind that one pictures oily from, say, engine parts, crude and threatening. Not that Harry's hands lacked power, but it was of another sort. Long slender fingers, deft and agile, never clumsy, attached to the fine bones of his hand, tanned flesh over blue veins, colours that blend delicately and well. And ending at the wrists, the prominent, sticking-out bones of the wrists, a dusting of pale hair. Discreet hands. Protecting and capable hands. Hands that knew and saw and did. Hands that would know me and take care. Hands that, put to other uses, would provide for us. It seemed to me that what was in his mind flowed into them, and they expressed his knowledge. They were the instruments of who he was. And of who we were, too.

Sometimes in the evenings I picked them up, just to gaze. Simply look. Wonder at their lines, which deepened, and their length and grace, at what they did in the hours that I did not see, at their authority and sureness. Harry lay in his hands for me.

(But the other places his hands went, that I did not know. Betraying hands.)

My own hands I look at with some astonishment. They are small and somewhat plump, pale, not stretched or taut like his. These hands, which have done so many small things and one large, great thing. A mystery, the history of these hands.

They have washed so many dishes and pushed a vacuum cleaner so many times. They have wiped so many cloths over so many windows, and their fingernails have scratched at so many small stains. They have scrubbed vegetables and peeled them, and they have carried hot things from the stove to the counter to the table. They have picked flowers from the garden, and tins from grocery shelves. They have stitched torn seams and pressed irons over crumpled cloth. They have lifted pillows to make them plump again, and heavy bags of groceries. They have turned pages and mattresses. I know they must be strong, but they are also docile, dutiful. They have almost always done what they were supposed to.

All those little things these hands did, I know each task wasn't so important. But I thought that taken together they must be. I thought they would protect us, build a perfect wall. Pictures I have seen of old cities: built inside great high impenetrable walls, so that no enemies could invade, and the citizens inside could go about their lives without the burden of fear. The walls that made them safe, as long as they stayed inside.

Outside the walls, of course, where the men went, danger. Wild animals, wild enemies, leaping to claw and kill. But then safe again inside, the letting out of breath, the loosening of tense muscles, the putting up of feet. Those walls, impractical in our day, could be recreated, the sense of them, in clean floors and dishes and well-cooked meals and vacuumed carpets, gleaming windows. Or so my hands believed.

So his hands went out and mine stayed in, and together, only four hands necessary for this, two of his, two of mine, we played ring-around-a-rosy in a closed circle, just the two of us.

(Except that one of his hands was busy elsewhere, and we had only three.)

It should have worked. There was a flaw there somewhere, but I can't tell what it was.

Maybe that my hands, for all I tried, did not go far enough. Things must be kept in order. A single small thing out of order must throw the whole structure faintly off its balance, and these things pile up.

If I see a pin on this floor, for instance, and fail to pick it up, what then? The next day, or the next hour, suddenly there is another pin, perhaps some fluff fallen from the blanket, God knows what else. If again I fail to pick up these things, more gather, and more, and they grow and grow until there is too much to pick up, and I am trapped in them. The thing must be to learn that when the pin is spotted, right then it must be taken and put in a place.

My failure before must surely have been in not going far enough. I took care of what I thought was small enough, but it was not. The chairs sat in the right places, the tables were dusted and polished, the drapes hung as they should, and behind them the hidden windowsills were wiped and white. There were no secret dirty places.

And still that wasn't enough. I was wrong to think the details could get no tinier. There must have been pins in the carpet that I did not see, and bits of lint on my dresses. There must have been a small stain on one of his ties that became blood.

My mother, unlikely for her, gave me wise advice. "Keep on top of things," she said, "never let them get ahead of you, it just makes extra work eventually." That made sense, and confirmed my instinct. But she did not warn me how far I would have to go. Did she not know? If she did not know, surely all the tiny unseen things would have had to rise together to trap her finally too? But they did not, apparently. Or did she know? If she did, it was unfair not to tell me. Her warnings did not go far enough.

All these tiny things. It is necessary, then, to live with the head down, watching?

So it would seem. And if I'd realized, I would have been quite happy to comply. I wanted badly to do the right thing. I wanted so badly to be good.

His hands did much broader jobs than mine. In his office, I imagine, they moved swiftly and competently over sheets of paper, his strong, dark, large, powerful handwriting scratching out his commands. So assured, those hands; knowing what must be done, doing it.

Hands gripped at home to the handles of the lawn mower; holding firm the vibrations of the roto-tiller as he prepared for flowers; wrapped sternly around the slippery green of plastic garbage bags; turning the pages of newspapers with a crackle, quick and precise, so that they folded as they ought, no fumbling or shuffling. Hands deftly manipulating corkscrews, opening wine bottles swiftly, cleanly, all these things done naturally, without great effort or concentration, part of his hands' skills.

Graceful hands that rolled paint in broad strokes and did not tremble around window edges. Hands that applauded for special meals, a smiling mouth above, appreciating my work with generosity.

(But I do not want to see his mouth. Or his eyes. Nothing more than his hands, which should say everything. But do not, any more.)

The hands, they do not change in memory. The rest much altered.

Hands (this is hard) that held my shoulders so that I was straight; and that folded themselves around my back so that I was safe. Hands that touched freely places in me hidden to every other person, hands I trusted to do that.

Oh, the lying hands. That they could do so many things so well and never tell. "Let not your right hand know what your left hand is doing," the Bible says, more or less. And I was Harry's right hand. He even told me that. He said, "I don't know what I'd do without you. I don't know what I might have been. You are my right hand." Also, at various times, his heart and his support. I could only show love; he could tell it, too, that was a power he had, dim lights and darkness, strong hands and whispered words. If I'd had words, what could I have said? Enough to hold his hands, to hold the circle closed and tight? But in my labour in the small things, surely my devotion spoke?

He said, "You take such good care of me." I know he was busy; people told me how hard he worked, how efficiently, how well, they said he was spectacular and tough. His promotions were a sign. He came home tense and vivid, and we shared a drink before dinner, and he looked around our perfect living room, all shined and cleaned and plumped and neat, and said, "God, it's good to be home." He made a second drink and read his newspaper. We had dinner. I wanted perfect textures in the food, and perfect colours. He noticed and said, "It's so pretty I hate to eat it." I did more than cook and serve, much more. I arranged. I was an artist. I created his home. I sketched each moment of the day with care, so that the portrait of his desires was precise when he arrived.

And his hands went around me.

I thought there were no spaces through which any of our care could dart or seep away, but some hole must have come uncovered, there was a leak.

Oh, that is some lesson. Hands or walls, not to be given faith. A hole will develop somewhere in a wall, and a searching, tempted hand poke through. With mere curiosity? Whatever. Hands lie, words lie. A little lie is like a little silver pin, it too adds up and expands.

But I believed. My faith was real, no lie.

Harry, though — his hands did not move independently of him. Oh no, he knew what his hands were up to.

Did he look at them sometimes and wonder at what they were capable of? I look at mine that way sometimes. They seem so innocent and placid now; difficult to believe what they have done. Yes, I can see Harry looking at his and feeling that way sometimes too.

3

DOES THIS MEAN I THOUGHT IT OUT and knew what I was doing? I'd like to think so, but it's past lies now. It turns out I spent twenty years unwittingly. Who taught me what to do, so that I thought it was my own idea?

And then I did a lifetime's thinking in a mere twelve hours, almost precisely twelve hours. The time between the phone call from that woman — what was her name, Dottie something? — and Harry coming home. An abrupt change of gears, a wrenching out of order in my life.

And Harry coming home. And a single clarifying moment.

I was upstairs vacuuming; twice a week I did each room. I have read of ground-in dirt, deep in carpet fibres, causing rot. Heard the phone, shut off the vacuum to be sure, dropped it, ran down the stairs, fit, quite fit for running, work and exercise have kept the body firm, to catch the fourth, maybe the fifth ring.

"Edna?" Not an unfamiliar voice, but also not one that could be placed exactly. "It's Dottie. Dottie Franklin." Yes, that's her name. What kind of person can she be?

"Are you busy? Have I called at a bad time?" She was just the wife, known casually, socially, of a man with whom Harry worked, whom Harry had beaten for the most recent promotion. She never called. Drinking? Perhaps; some lonely women did. Not I, I had no reason.

"Edna, this is difficult." Not drunk; tension, not liquor, in the voice.

"It's something Jack saw this morning on his way to work. Just by accident because our car wouldn't go and he had to get a ride with some man at the garage and the guy took a different route."

So?

I saw my knuckles, holding the receiver, turn white. I felt my body tighten and my mind turn cold. Ice in my warm and perfect home.

"It was only eight o'clock in the morning. There couldn't be any other explanation. I'm sorry, Edna, but I thought you ought to know. It's only fair."

Fair? What the hell is fair? Is knowledge more fair than faith? More valuable? Oh, God would have done better to make me Eve than the Eve He made. I would not have chosen knowledge over peace.

I don't think I would have.

Once knowing, there is no going back.

"What can I say, Edna? Forgive me, I had to let you know."

The wallpaper in the living room was fairly new. Gold-flecked white. Elegant, I thought, for just one wall. I'd done it in a day, and when Harry came home he put an arm around me and said, "Lovely. Just right. I was afraid it would be too pale but you knew best, as usual." He did not say that resentfully, but with pride in my judgment and taste. In my home I did not make mistakes, and he would have been surprised, no doubt, if the wallpaper had not been right.

So. The wallpaper before me, the carpet beneath my feet clean, the pillows around me on the couch all pure. The gold flecks danced in the wallpaper.

My house was always quiet. Any sounds in the day were only mine, and I liked that. But this was a different stillness, a different sort of waiting.

It seemed to me that I had never moved, could never have; that I had only ever waited. And that there was just this motionless instant, only this; the ends of my life snapped off, leaving this moment of waiting in the centre.

Broken again at one point by the telephone. Answered

without taking my eyes from the gold-flecked whiteness of the wall, the point that rooted, the point without which I might topple, slide, lose balance irrevocably. Groped for the receiver.

"Edna?" Harry, of course. His dear, familiar voice, warm along the line. But so distant. Like going deaf, a faint tinkling of burning words. "Listen, I'm sorry but I'm going to have to work late again. This job is driving me crazy, there's a lot more to it than I thought. Do you mind? I should make it by midnight anyway. I'm sorry, there's nothing I can do about it."

No, maybe not.

Twelve hours I had between that woman's call and the moment Harry appeared. I heard his car, his key, his steps, running water in the bathroom, the flushing of the toilet, more footsteps from above, a calling, shouting, quick movement down the stairs; steps to the kitchen, then into the living room where I sat, holding on to my vision's place in that wall of gold-flecked white. Saw his handsome, well-known, well-loved face before me, coming between me and the wall. And as I had thought, a toppling, dizziness, no balance.

Later I watched the clock on the kitchen wall, white, shaped like a daisy, with a yellow centre and yellow hands, and the yellow hand that showed the seconds went around and around so slowly, slowly, time all finished in twelve hours and then an instant. Two-eighteen in the morning. Two-nineteen, two-twenty. Over by then. The twelve hours and the moment, done.

I did not look. I never saw the result.

4

THE MAN WHO COMES SOMETIMES to my room, to whose office I am sometimes led, the doctor, his hands are much like Harry's. I find myself staring at them, and once he said, "You seem interested in my hands. Is there something about them?"

Yes, there is. But I do not tell him. I guard my thoughts. I am forty-three years old, and I have had, it appears, only twelve hours' worth of thoughts, so I have to cherish them. I do not have so many that some can be given away.

Nor do I want any of them to slip my mind, which is one reason I take such care to write them down. The man, this doctor, says, "Edna, what do you write? Will you show me the notebook?" No, of course I will not do that. He tried, one day, to make me; reached out to stop my pen, so that a blue slash cut across all my careful neatness, but I put a stop to that: the pen turned in my hand, wrist as quick as a baton-twirler's, and my hand went up, pen aimed at him like — some other thing — and he fell back, gave in, said, "Don't be upset, go ahead, it's all right."

This notebook, it is a lot like that gold-flecked wall-paper: it helps me keep my balance. It also keeps at a distance all the other things that are going on, that have already gone on. I desire that distance, appreciate the gaps between what all this is, what was, and me. I may have been blind, naïve, but I am not now.

The doctor, he talks on and on and I know he thinks he is going to reach me. This blue notebook is my weapon against that. Past pain and present pain are neatly filed in here, and that is what it's for. I am coming to the end of the first notebook and soon will ask for a second. How many will there be? How many years can I live?

With the doctor I am a stenographer, noting carefully his words. But without shorthand, in my own neat script, hurrying to keep up and struggling still for tidiness. This is not easy, but it is easier than other things.

He tells me about his wife and his two children, and about his house. I see that he is trying to draw me out. He wants to make me share my life by sharing his. But his words fall into the well of my notebook like stones, and they just lie there, flat.

He asks me questions. "How are you feeling today? Are you comfortable? Is everybody treating you all right? Are you happy with the meals?"

I write down his questions.

He asks so many. Sometimes he tries to make me use the notebook for his purpose, and says, "Write me a story about your house. Or draw me a picture. Tell me what it looked like. Was it big? What colour was it? Show me how the rooms were laid out. Was there a garage? Did it hold one car or two? What colour was the kitchen? Did you make your own curtains? Was the basement finished? Did Harry do work in the basement? Where did you watch television? Did you watch much television? What sort of programs did you like? How many phones did you have? Did you keep your cookbooks on the kitchen counter, or did you have a special shelf for them? How many bedrooms were there? Did you and Harry share one? Did you have twin beds or a big one? Did you and Harry sleep together in the same bed? Did you like to be in bed? What colour were your sheets?"

I tell him nothing. Not even the colour of the sheets. It's not his business. I like the sound of my pen scratching across the page. Sometimes I hear it so clearly it almost drowns out his voice, with his endless questions.

Still, here they are, all written down.

Yes, our house was quite big; foolishly big for just the

two of us, although it was early when we bought it, and we thought there might be more. Three bedrooms, two bathrooms, an enormous basement for laundry, storage, furnace, Harry's hobbies, if he had had any — a gaping dark space beneath us. And on the main floor, brightness and big rooms, stairways to the up and down, a gleaming, a shining, and pastels on the walls. Lightness and solidity. A magazine could have come and taken photographs and would have called it typical, but it was more to me: the place, haven, where our lives were led, disregarding Harry's life outside. Should I not have seen how much of his was beyond that small and narrow space? That for all its size, it in no way contained him? It contained me, and I could not imagine, although he told me so much, that truly he existed when he left the house. He went out in the morning and came back at night, and all that was a mystery, while I prepared for his return.

I might have known, for he talked about his days, of deals and negotiations, labyrinthine relationships of office politics and promotions. He said, "Damn, Edna, I love to win," and he would be flushed and trembling with his passion. And me, I thought (how stupidly) that that could not really be his passion; that truly it must be in our home. I could not imagine any other passion but my own.

I listened and encouraged, but I did not hear. There are two faults of mine: that protective deafness, that failure of imagination.

I ramble, and that's dangerous.

Yes, there was a garage attached to our house. Room for a single car. I have not learned to drive. I walked to the convenience store nearby, took taxis downtown when I was to meet Harry for an evening out, and for the rest he drove me, in the evenings or on the weekends, when there were errands to be done. He did not seem to mind. I liked those times when we were together doing the small things that were necessary; so that our household was more firmly ours and he had something to do with it. I could sit beside him in the car and watch him, his profile alert to other drivers, other cars, watching for spaces in the plazas, handling so easily, as he did so many things, the steering wheel, casually one-handed, the other hooked to the chrome ledge above the window, flicking turn signals. My confident, capable husband. Saturday expeditions for food, paint, even merely lightbulbs, an outing, and I could sit beside him in our closed steel car and wonder at his ease, catch my breath at his daring, his risks with the body of the car and our own bodies as he nipped in and out of narrow spaces, cursing but not disliking the chores by any means: relishing the challenge of defeating another driver, racing, beating him to a small goal, the entrance to a mall, a parking spot in front of a store, his weekend challenges. A restless, pacing man; he wanted to be active, doing, and so I did not feel it was a burden that he had to drive me to these places.

Difficult, however, in a store, where he was impatient, did not care for careful choosing, wanting to be done and on to the next thing. While I, humming to the piped music, dazzled by fluorescent lights and people, crowds, could happily drift among the aisles picking, comparing, discarding, watching.

Harry used to say, "Christ, do we really spend all this on food?" Well yes, we spent a great deal on food. It's neither inexpensive nor simple to buy for meals that don't just taste good in the ordinary way, but are also beautiful to look at. Broccoli must be a certain green, and firm, and roasts must have a particular amount of fat marbled through. You have to examine closely to make sure there are no grey edges. You have to squeeze lettuce and hold fruits, heft them, close your eyes to feel the texture of their interior, and even smell them. Some cheeses are for sauces, others for snacks, and for each purpose age, consistency, and colour must be considered. This is a skill, judging the quality of food and its beauty, making plans that foresee its end, how its parts will contrast and blend on the plate and lead properly to dessert. No conflicting colours or tastes. Against all this, price was no consideration. We were not poor, there was no necessity to pick and choose that way. And, in any case, on these shopping days Harry would be off down another aisle, feet tapping, amusing himself by examining content lists on cereals and cookies, always ready to be moving on. I worked my way along with care and what speed was possible. Aware of his impatience. If I was so alert to his impatience, why not to other things? In twenty years, in even a single year, I thought I could feel each of his moods and irritations. And yet missed the vital one. How could that have been?

Home again, on a weekend afternoon, unloading the car, doors hanging open while we did so, waiting while he journeyed up the stone walk edged with borders of chrysanthemums and shrubs, into our pale yellow house, our pale yellow kitchen, where I put away the things we bought as Harry carried them in.

In daylight, I think, we were both restless, active. But he from an excess of energy, a twitching in the fingers, eager to be doing; I because accustomed to things having to be done, completed, by the time dark came. Difficult to break the compulsions of the week when the week was finished.

But in darkness both of us more placid, more satisfied, things finished, so that we could settle with wine and dinner, an evening reading, watching television, curled together on the couch, which was best, or settled separately to our own amusements, which was not my choice. I did know things, however: from magazines learned that some privacy must be granted, one must not cling. Hard to follow that advice. I would have liked to curl my arms around his neck and hang from it, but did not dare; instead sat watching him; myself reading, or watching television, but still glancing at him often. How were we together? How did he find me and why did he choose me? Oh, I owed him everything. My life, I owed to Harry.

Did he owe me anything? Whatever, he paid.

How remote those days seem now. How wonderful and

cherishable eventlessness is. It is most precious, living without drama, with certainty. I remember and it is so far away, detached and foreign, that it is like watching another person's life, and I am filled with wonder at all that was once possible. I wish I had known and appreciated. I did appreciate, but not enough and not in the proper ways. I would give much, now, for a day, a week, a month, a year, a life, in which nothing of great importance happens. I would know how to relish its safety properly.

What would I do with Harry, if I could have all that again?

No, I did not sew any of our curtains. When we bought that house, I wanted everything to be just right, and so ordered drapes and curtains, men coming to measure and install, hanging them precisely, the exact shades and nuances for each room, bright cheerful yellow for the kitchen, golden for the living room, heavy material shielding rooms from watchers, sheers beneath for filtering out bright light; upstairs in the bedrooms, more matching — blue in the bedroom of Harry and myself, same as the carpet, the walls, a perfect womb. White-shaded lamps on dark wood bedside tables, dark wood bed, dark wood dresser, and all the rest blue. I can see Harry, propped up on the pillows, gold-rimmed glasses slipping on his nose (this in the later years, eyes a little weakened, bifocals required and his anxiety about that, the concern behind the joke: "Oh Edna, you're married to an old man now"), reading reports from the office, books. He was not one for novels, although I was. He said, "I haven't time. There's too much going on that's real." He liked biographies of successful men, and business reports. I preferred the gentler fiction. I thought, "I'm sure there's as much truth, as much that's real," but had nothing to compare it with, no way to say if that was accurate. Maybe he was right and my books were false and fairy tales. They did seem hopeful, showed possibilities of happy endings, and maybe it was wrong of me to believe in them.

I am sad and puzzled by things misinterpreted, misunderstood, unseen, and missed.

Because I was so sure. How could I have been so sure, and so wrong? Was I so very wrong? Is it not possible that most of it was true and only one thing not? But if so, could that one thing ever have existed? I do not understand.

Magazines, and I have read so many, plucked from supermarket shelves in check-out lines, insist on the complexity of men. They counsel patience. I was a patient woman, I believe; but now see that that was largely my own nature and had little to do with Harry.

What good is it to know these things now?

I cannot say. But I keep busy, I write on.

Yes, Harry and I shared a bed, double-sized. The sheets were blue, the beautiful intricate quilted family gift, the only beautiful thing that ever came from my parents' home, spread over them. I cannot think of that.

I feel here as if I do not really exist. The way it used to be on evenings when Harry could not get home (would not get home) and I was alone and watching, maybe, television. I liked my days alone, so much to do. But in the evenings, in the dark, it was different, lonely. It seemed to me abnormal, freakish, to be alone at night — unwanted. It brought back too many fears.

Television, that was some company. Not so much the programs, but the idea that these were people acting. And what was behind it? A strained comic, the father, maybe, of a crippled child? The husband of a faithless wife? These were the things that interested me.

But if I thought of hidden things on television, why not in my home? The drama less apparent. Not obvious at all that this also was not real, and that there were also hidden things.

Here, in this dry place that is not my home, the unreal is what there is. It makes me feel as if I'm floating off somewhere and might float off forever, without this anchor of my body to the chair, my ankles neatly crossed, the notebook precisely in my lap, the pen moving neatly across the pages, following the lines.

This cannot be what is happening. But it is.

I would give anything to go back. To undo and do again. I am blinded by knowing it is not possible. It should be possible. I would be so much better, knowing what I know. I would be perfect. If I were perfect (I thought I was, but now perceive the cracks), would he not be also? And then all of this unnecessary. Unreal, impossible.

5

I SEE MY FACE, my body, in the mirror. In the morning, I need merely sit up straight in bed to see me staring back.

And other starings, too. This face is forty-three years old, and there are many more faces than just this one. There is a child, a young girl, an adolescent, and all the ages of the married woman. Each has contributed to the face I see now, much the way you see on TV shows, a police composite of a suspect added to with sheets of plastic, each lined with different features. It builds up that way, the face you get.

I have spent hours looking into mirrors; and yet I don't know if I would recognize myself, if I met me in the hall or on a street. The way I now see Harry, maybe: fragmented, bits here and there. I know that my nose is slightly too large. My mouth, which I'm sure was once a little fuller, is now pulled somewhat tight. Blue eyes; nothing much to be said for or against them; they're normal-sized and no extraordinary colour and a normal distance from each other. Nothing is grotesque about me, nothing is unusual, and I suppose that's the effect I've tried for with all the time and money and effort I've invested in it. I wanted to stay young and firm, I thought, for Harry; but maybe for myself as well? I cared for him the best ways I knew how, and I kept myself trim and attractive. Or not unattractive. Oh, I read the magazines, I knew what was required.

But did I not have my own fear of aging? Was it just to do with Harry? I peered into mirrors and saw the tense tracings of new lines around the eyes, the mouth, and had despairing visions of a loosening throat and saggings.

I fought with exercises every day, stretching muscles and flattening belly, tightening thighs; tap-tapping at my chin with the back of my hand a hundred times a day, fending off extra flesh. I had coffee for breakfast and a small salad for lunch, and shared the dinner I made for Harry. As if I were a race horse, I groomed and trained myself.

When I washed my face, or massaged it with creams and lotions, I did so with upward motions, never down, a consciousness and then a habit of encouraging skin to reach up, not down.

Nor have I done badly. There are those lines and a few grey hairs sprouting amid the brown. I have never weighed more than a hundred and fifteen pounds, and suspect I may be smaller now. I do not have spreading hips or drooping thighs. "Lovely ass," Harry used to say, passing by and patting me. I could still wear shorts in the summer.

I found my first grey hair before I was thirty, and was a little stunned to see the change beginning. But really, it hasn't gotten much worse.

My breasts are still quite firm, despite a few small tension marks up where they begin. My belly is a little fleshy, no longer quite flat, but then, I would think that might even be a bit attractive: warm, a small pillow which might seem a place to rest.

There are freckles, but not unsightly, on my arms. On the back of my left arm, above the elbow, there's a small and harmless mole. If I were found dead on a street with no papers in my purse, they would have trouble, I think, identifying me by marks on the body. They would have to look for dental records, and even there, only some anonymous fillings.

I can see creases in my skin, around my waist, behind my knees, and despite all my efforts, little flesh-drawings around my throat. If I look closely I can examine the pores of my calves from which hairs sprout. They do not, of course, give me the use of a razor, but an aide comes along to shave the hair occasionally. She does it quickly, but doesn't tear the skin. "My, Mrs. Cormick, you have shapely legs," she says. She is quite young; no doubt that's why she sounds surprised.

How old was she? I paid so little attention. Maybe twenty-six or twenty-seven? Not even beautiful. If she were beautiful, or important, I might have noticed, might have seen that she had gifts that I did not. But there seemed nothing remarkable about her.

Was that his taste, then?

I can see a strain about the body and the face in the mirror, but that is understandable.

But shouldn't there be something more in a face that's almost forty-four? Should I not at least be able to see it clearly? Where are its powers? I don't mean lines, anyone can have lines. I mean a sharpness, clarity. There should be something that says, "I have lived forty-three years, I have existed." The mirror should have something to say.

Instead I feel small and obscure, like a vase, or a photograph on the wall, and my face seems white and infirm, too soft, unnatural, like a kind of cool putty.

There are three lines crossing my forehead, fairly deep ones, no way to ever massage them away; and there are two other deep ones alongside my mouth, one on each side. Around my eyes there's a little darkness, a brown-grey tinge that makes me look like one of those Arab women who seek that shade for emphasis, or mystery. I feel, peering, like an old watercolour and expect to see cracks like dried paint break across my face.

6

WHEN I WAS A LITTLE GIRL, I had a full-length mirror in my bedroom. Evenings, when I was supposed to be in bed, I posed before it; practised walking, prancing, standing hand on hip, tilted backward, mimicking advertisements in my mother's magazines, those models selling dresses and cosmetics.

"Am I pretty?" I wondered. "How pretty am I?" I couldn't tell. Even then, I failed to quite see myself.

Strange, because I could certainly tell about others. People on the street, one knew at a glance whether they were pretty or not. My little sister Stella, born three years after me, anyone could see that she was. People said to my parents, "What lovely little girls," but perhaps they were taking an average? Balancing beautiful Stella against plain Edna and coming up with a comprehensive lovely? How could I tell if this was what was happening?

My hair grew long, my mother cut it short, it grew again, it fluffed and bristled with childhood permanents or hung lank. I had bangs, let them grow out, and had them recut — and at each change I peered into the mirror, wondering at the differences, wondering if they made enough difference. "Am I pretty?"

I suppose not. Surely anyone who is can tell. They can look and see perfect features and know, it must be as obvious as seeing that one is ugly. I was sure that if I were ugly, I would know that, also, at a glance. Therefore, somewhere in the middle: disappointed to be not lovely, but relieved also to be not ugly.

Anything striking about me, then, would have to be manufactured. But that risks garishness and foolishness.

Even now I would like to think these things don't matter. It would be nice to think that one is assessed for virtues only. But not even the teachers liked the fat boys, and no one wanted to be seen with the girl with the glasses, poor clothes, the dark and greasy cast of skin. Certainly I did not want to be seen with her; one would be afraid of being viewed as her reflection.

No, a good appearance was essential, the first thing people saw and how they judged. It was obvious that it determined, was first cause, of how a life would go. It might be a mask for some other truth beneath the flesh, but people did not look for truth that way. Even a child knew that. Even the child Edna knew that a display of fear or pain would mar the surface.

And there were other things even a child would know. The proper pattern of a life, how it should be led, this knowledge was absorbed. One was a girl and so inevitably would become a woman and the way to be followed was well laid out and obvious. To wander off was failure. I considered my mother a failure in this way, a mutant of a woman. An embarrassment.

Before we were married, Harry tried and tried to make me talk. He'd say, "I'm not going to say a word, Edna. I'm just going to sit here until you say something." Or he'd ask me questions about myself.

When I met him, I could barely speak.

He said, "Tell me about your family, Edna." This was before he met them.

What I thought was that they were entirely the wrong way about. Why did my mother buy those magazines, when she obviously had no intention of following their advice?

The magazines and books, the world itself outside our own, showed clearly that the real and normal system was the reverse of the one in our home. My parents unaccountable aberrations.

I see my mother. The last time I saw her, some months ago now, I guess, she was a bit stooped, but still angular and hard. As a child I stood below her and looked up her long plank of a body and knew that in a contact with her I would be hurt. Even a hug when I was small and soft and she was tall and hard was dangerous.

She made my father smoke outdoors and would not let him drink. He went out to the porch or the backyard to smoke his pipe. I don't know where he went to drink, but sometimes he came home silly, and she would slam plates and doors.

But I thought, "Well, why shouldn't he? Why shouldn't he be able to do what he wants?" He was so quiet most of the time, except when he was silly. He worked in a hardware store and handed her his pay each week. She gave him back a little for his spending.

He couldn't have known before they were married. So she must have betrayed him during their courtship with some other face, a lie.

"Sit up straight," she said to me. (To Stella, too, no doubt.) "Don't get dirty." "Clean up your plate."

I never heard them quarrel, and I also never saw them kiss. It was strange, with Harry, to have him so different; he liked his hands to be touching something.

My mother's dresses hung awkwardly. She took long strides. She wore my father's rubber boots outside to hang the wash.

And yet. I admit they grew to fit, whether they started that way or not. Who else, as they turned out to be, could either of them have lived with? And maybe she would have liked sometimes to wear pretty dresses and dainty shoes, to say, "Dear, your supper's ready," or "How nice, you got a raise, you must be doing well." Maybe she would have liked it if he'd managed something. It was sad, her bitterness and his defeat.

It was also an example. I set myself to be quite different. I paid attention to the magazines and not my mother, and pledged that when I married (however that would come about; but it had to), I would cherish the state properly.

And so I did. And now I don't know how things ought to work, I really don't.

She must have done something truly strange to make my father so invisible. I imagined her burned as a witch for her skill at transformations. What else might she do?

So I hid my own face from her, for fear that if she saw it, if I displayed a need, she might make me disappear as well. It was a good deal safer to be silent and off to one side. When I fell down outside and skinned my knees, I stopped the blood with leaves and had a quiet, private weep. I did not go crying to her to have her kiss it better. (But such an exaggerating child I must have been, because of course she would have comforted me, she was not so unnatural.)

Then I saw her sometimes with her friends, who would come for tea in the afternoon when my father was at work, and she was somewhat different: smiled and talked and crossed her legs comfortably and let her shoulders down a little; was this the face she'd used to win my father?

I thought about her quite a lot in those days, and understood my own intentions.

This is not her fault, though, what has happened and where I am. It's just that that was such a tiny world, our house and that small town. Only the magazines brought news of the outside and I devoured them for clues.

Such a relief and a revelation Harry was, a man who spoke, apparently, all his thoughts, even bits of meanness, so that of course I believed he was a truthful man and showed me everything. The only person I could take at what they call face value. I loved him for that, although I would have loved him anyway, for giving me a life.

It was my mother who said I had to go to university; my father merely acquiesced. "You're smart enough, Edna," she said, and it was true my marks were good, or good enough, better than Stella's, at any rate. I was never stupid that way. "You can make something of yourself."

I heard the bitterness in her voice, but then, I often heard bitterness in her voice and didn't pay attention.

I don't even know if she liked me or loved me. She did seem to want things from me, though.

However did they manage to have Stella and me? Especially the unaccountable Stella, who seemed to belong to another family entirely?

Stella, who cried so hard both of them went to her, who shouted and defied and tossed her head and went freely, not caring, out the door when she wanted to. She bowled them over with the volume of her demands.

I mean only that we were quite different, not that I disliked my sister.

They were my family. When I went away, I expect I missed them. Among all the strangers in the world, they knew me best.

They haven't come to see me here, nor have they written. Do they hate me now, do I frighten them, or are they just not allowed to come or write?

They must be terribly bewildered and ashamed, I imagine. More than anybody else, except of course for Harry's parents, they must wonder why.

They must all have wept, and mourned for one thing or another.

"Dear Edna," my mother-in-law once said to me, patting my shoulder, "you're so good for Harry."

7

I EVEN PRACTISED KISSING with that full-length mirror in my bedroom: long, passionate twistings of lips against cool, smooth glass. Trying to see how it might be.

I thought, "Some day, this is really going to happen," but couldn't imagine. He was tall and dark but had no face.

I progressed to embraces with my pillow, more responsive. Practising again: one would hate, when the time came, to be clumsy or not know how.

But was it possible the mirror and the pillow would be all there ever was?

No, this could not be possible, however unimaginable it might be, getting there from here.

I experimented with lipstick and mascara, rouge and powder. I checked the growth of my breasts, wanting them large enough to mould desirability beneath blouses and sweaters, but not so large as to be vulgar. At a certain point, they stopped growing and I was pleased.

It was all so *difficult*. I watched amazed as Stella, three years after me, moved so gracefully, easily, into all the places that caused me pain.

Standing by a wall in the high school auditorium, waiting to be asked to dance, waiting and waiting. Watching the others, wondering how it worked. I really thought (I still think) they knew some secret, those people with their shining skin and laughter, their swinging hair and flinging arms, their shuffling, leaping feet. There was some secret that they all knew and that nobody had told me and that nobody would ever tell me. And it showed, that I didn't know.

I smiled and smiled. My face hurt with the smiling. A

band of boys, classmates, but they looked different up there on the stage, playing Presley: "Don't Step on My Blue Suede Shoes." I moved my body to the rhythm and tapped my feet and kept on smiling, but that was not the secret. Those others, agile on the dance floor, did not step on each other's shoes (not blue suede but white pumps, or saddle shoes with white ankle socks). When the music turned slow, girls laid their heads on boys' shoulders and something steamy seemed to rise from the floor.

I couldn't help watching.

Home, I turned again to my pillow. If I were part of two, I understood, I would be inside and able to look out, instead of the reverse. Being held, that must be something.

I kissed the pillow. "Good night, dear," I whispered. "Sleep well."

Ah, Harry was so beautiful. He saved my life.

I never told him that. It would have terrified him.

He used to say, "Edna, loosen up. Nobody's going to bite." Not true. I never had faith that someone wouldn't, gleaming teeth lurching from the crowd, gripping my too-free wrist.

And I was right, after all. Even the most-loved people slash like animals under certain circumstances.

I thought, "Maybe if I watch carefully, I'll see what the secret is." This involved not being watched myself. I preferred in any case to go unnoticed, until I could work it out. Because if people were looking, might I not make them laugh by doing something awkward or foolish? A pimple on my chin would blaze at them if they were looking, whereas if they were not, it would go quietly away. If I stumbled or lost the trail of a sentence when I spoke, was it not better if no one was listening?

Certainly it was better to hold my hands at my sides than to reach out and risk a blow.

It is very peculiar to have done so much in the interests of safety and wind up in this position.

And then, along behind me came Stella. Pretty, assured,

gay, and laughing Stella. Oh, weeping and rebellious Stella, too, but so what? It was all simple for her.

However did she manage to become a Stella in that house? That dark, sad house where even the smells were damp and heavy; that house where despair and grimness and disappointment and impatience warred to become the theme of each day. Where the couch and chairs were dark brown, nubbly and cheap, and the curtains were heavy and lined, and all the wood was painted over and as brown as the furniture. Where wallpaper had light colours but heavy designs, great green flowers and ferns slammed onto white so that it was a wonder they stayed up; so cumbersome one might expect to get up one morning and find a heap of paper greenery tumbled on the floor.

We were not so poor. It was not as ugly as my memory conjures it. It was the atmosphere that darkened it, more than wood and walls, the atmosphere that was damp and heavy and sucked away my courage and any words I might have had. I was inclined to creep about it quietly, like a frightened bug.

But Stella came out of the same house. How does one account for that?

How does she remember the house where we grew up?

I watched with amazement the ease with which she met people, the ease with which she found words to fill hours on the telephone, the ease with which her hair fell bouncing into place. Boys knocked shyly on the door and she flung away with them into the bright night on her dates, with just a happy "Good-bye, see you later." I listened to the radio with my parents.

Whatever the secret was, she knew it.

My parents never said, "Look at Stella, how popular she is, why aren't you?" They didn't have to say that: we all knew, spending our evenings silently and helplessly together. I lay on the couch with my eyes closed and the radio delivered music and stories. I breathed evenly and did not move, but in my head I sang songs with the bands and whirled around polished dance floors with some dark and handsome man. I was the singer and the dancer and the heroine of all the stories. With my eyes closed, I could vanish.

I wore long red silk dresses and flowers in my hair, and was much older than I was. But beautiful. Or was a torch singer in a dress of simple black, a spotlight shining on me and all the rest in darkness. I held my hand to my heart in a play and said, "Oh yes, I love you, of course I'll marry you." Men wanted my attention and thrust roses at me on the stage. My voice was a miracle, my body filled with grace. I was warm and charming and knew what to say. I was praised and perfect and lovely. And was aware, although it was not evident on the stage, that in my own bright home was a handsome man who loved me and was waiting for me with a glass of wine and long, embracing arms.

Oh, it was a perfect life, with everything. My own days were, in contrast, drab and there were times when I could hardly wait for evening and for Stella to leave (although if I'd been asked, I would have dashed out just like her, off to parties and dances and movies, of course I would have) and for my parents to settle and turn on the radio, to rejoin that perfect life in which people looked at me with such admiration and I was a gifted, lovely, much-loved woman. And said such things with my body and my voice, all the things that otherwise would go unsaid.

And then my father would stretch and yawn, the joints of his jaws and fingers cracking, and that world slammed shut and no matter if I was in the midst of a song there, or if the dance wasn't finished yet: back I was tossed into that small dark room where I lay still and silent on the couch. "Time to get to bed, young lady," he always said. "Early day tomorrow." Because it was always an early day for us, seven o'clock each weekday for school and work, eight o'clock on weekends for chores and church. When could I get out of this, and how would it come about? Who was the person who would find me here and whose eyes would recognize me and who would take me away to some life I belonged in?

Now there are just the two of them. And I suppose they watch television instead of listening to the radio.

And Stella's life has had its peculiar patches. There are things I would like to ask her about. I missed my chance, when one occurred, but now, for one reason and another, I seem to miss her. I would like it if she were to come and visit.

I go astray too often here, and occasionally too far. What I should be doing is keeping an eye on the carpet, and examining the bedspread.

8

BUT THERE I WAS, a lump of a frightened child, no way to tell if other people were frightened too, although now I suppose many of them must have been. One of the blindnesses of youth, that one thinks oneself unique, I guess, and fails to see the ways others hide themselves. All I knew was that I had several faces, all of them hidden, and multiple longings and couldn't tell which was true. And that there was that secret that, had I known it, would have made many things clear and different. It was a dangerous and vulnerable state, wandering about not knowing something others did. Who could tell the menaces of ignorance?

And yet there was something else I knew: that at some point there would be a change. I would be a different person entirely. It would come when I was no longer a child, when I left this house and this town, when I turned twenty.

I have my bits of tough, hard stubbornness. That faith that I would not always be a frightened child was one. I could think, "This will end, so it may not always be important. When I am twenty and different, it won't be important at all."

How sweet, and sad, remembering that hope, and twenty now so long ago.

I had no idea how the change would come about. A fairy godmother's wand-wave? Of course not, but something. It could not always be a matter of that small unpleasant house, or of mirrors and pillows only.

(And when change did come, I was so grateful that I never dared to hope for it again. What is given can equally be taken away, a paralysing possibility.)

It would be a matter of a man. Who would see beyond my plainness, or lack of loveliness, beyond my silence and my fear, to the woman in red singing and dancing on a stage. All the Ednas I contained, he would see and want. He would delight in my shyness, and protect me from my fear. He would hold me in the night and keep away the silence and the dark.

He would also stand up with me in daylight and say to people, "This is my wife." So there would be no confusion about who I was. Even for myself, it would be sorted out.

All this, which would happen when I was twenty and grown up, was as vivid, and as distant, as the other lives I led in the evenings with my eyes closed.

What magic did that number have for the child Edna? Then, it seemed impossibly old and distant. When I was in my teens, it began to glitter a little way ahead, in and out of view, shimmering on the horizon. From the faceless frightened girl would come the woman, leaping some mysterious gap; who would be the butterfly from the caterpillar, the graceful swan from the ugly duckling, and the heroine of all those other childhood stories.

Some effort would be involved. But while I was not at the time equipped for such an effort, and would probably not even recognize it, part of the magic of twenty was that then I would be capable of it, and of seeing it.

I saw my life patterned in numbers, a connect-the-dot puzzle in a child's magazine. A straight vertical line rising from the bottom, from birth to five; then a jog up and to the left to nine; vertical again to twelve; and then a long flat horizontal stretch to be trudged along to twenty. And there the lines might change, go anywhere, a new pattern might begin and who could tell where it might go once the leap was made?

But it must all go somewhere. I was a cherisher of lines and patterns.

And then I was nineteen and my mother was sending me off to university. "*Now* you'll do well, Edna," she said, with a surprising kindness, however tactless. I flushed at how clearly she must have seen that I had not been doing well at all.

But I shared her view. Now I would have to do well, because I was nineteen and twenty was very soon. So this was the preparation for the change.

Blind and frightened and anticipating, I stepped into space. There was no direction I could look to see anything at all. Back was painful and would become irrelevant; forward I could not yet imagine. It could be anything. Instead of looking, I hovered on the instant of the change.

My mother and Stella stood on the front porch and we all waved good-bye. My father drove me to the city and my own apartment we had found. "Well," he said, turning to leave, "that's it then, I guess," and kissed my cheek clumsily. I wanted for a moment to ask him to stay, to tell him I was frightened. But I was always frightened, and he couldn't stay, and if he did, what? He couldn't help, never had.

So I was finally alone. It seemed such a natural state that I barely noticed. A brief reprieve, a luxury before twenty, when something, a plunge into the real life I would have, must be accomplished.

I sound so helpless and full of pity for myself. But in fact, along with the frightened child I carried also that bone of determination. What else took me to those dances, to stand smiling and hoping and tapping my feet? What else could have taken me off alone to university, to that apartment where I cut pictures from magazines to brighten the walls? It is some accomplishment to suffer fear, but to plod on none the less. There is some pride in survival.

I wandered the city and the campus, watching. Great stone buildings there were, and acres of grass and flows of people like spawning salmon, hugging books to their chests or swinging briefcases. The classes were huge. One could be lost, which should make it easier to be brave. Who would notice?

"Just do well, Edna," my mother said before I left. "It isn't easy for us to afford this for you."

So I studied hard, went to all the classes and wrote essays and dragged books home from the library. But it turned out to be surprisingly easy. I had even then an eye for detail, an eye that picked up something, in those days a piece of knowledge, a fact, and held it for as long as it was needed. I don't suppose I learned, but I remembered.

And watched. A psychology professor had a laboratory of rats, and it was somewhat similar, seeing which way things ran in this unfamiliar place.

At nights I pulled a chair to the window of my apartment and watched the people passing on the sidewalk, sitting out on their porches for the last late-autumn warmth. They couldn't see me, sitting in the dark. They wouldn't have even thought to look. When I smell autumn now, I am returned to that window, breathing leaves.

And then very late, when everything was quiet and there was no more to watch, I shut the curtains and turned on the lights inside. Here I was safe and warm, alone, and although being alone could make me uneasy, it was also pleasant. No one could see.

I turned on the radio then, lay down on my makeshift couch, and became again the singers and the dancers. No father now to stretch and yawn and break the moment, and sometimes I fell asleep lying there and dreamed in the other lives, not my own.

Other lives were also offered up on bulletin boards. They lined the walls of corridors and I stood reading them. From advertisements for typing services to schedules of concerts and plays and notices of meetings, like a detective I tried to see which ones might leap out and offer a reward, a life.

They offered everything. A club for foreign students? The notice said anyone welcome, and I was as much a foreigner here as anyone. Did the round black faces, or the brown and aquiline, feel as removed from this as I did? I walked through the halls and across lawns, changing classes, and it was like someone else watching this.

Oh, the places these people would know, places I would

never see except in pictures in my mind. Wild colours and shapes of clothes, strange dances and music. Imagine, I thought, to see a desert. How would an infinity of nothing look? Here the eyes encountered intrusions — trees, or people, buildings. How would it be, seeing nothing?

How would dust be, or jungle? Hunger and the threat of death? One could imagine a black man who would sweep me up and take me home to be a princess. In a different world, I might be beautiful.

But then of course, faced with it, one might find it all quite different. At a meeting one might hear that seeing a desert was merely dull; that the threat of death only made one snappish; that the politics were small and human; that the life of a princess was confining.

I preferred an exotic, golden Timbuktu to what it more likely was, a hungry, dusty outpost.

Pictures in the mind are not unimportant, after all. I have spent considerable effort in my time, protecting pictures.

What I wanted was some grace, a wealth of spirit that would add, not take away. Some way, perhaps, to say what moved behind the eyelids: the dances and the songs.

And here I was on my own, out of the small, contained town and in a city which must have proportionately greater possibilities; where the right longings might be unleashed.

A literary magazine came out four times a year. One saw these people in the corridors, wearing black, some with wisps of beards, women with long straight hair pressed flat around pale faces, expressions drifting or defiant. The darkness of the foreign faces, the pallor of the literary ones — equally exotic, foreign, and attractive.

The magazine contained sad and gentle stories, outraged and bitter poems. About war, betrayal, pain, and poverty, but different: not politics and facts, but forms. And also about dim bodies, twisting and caressing. It seemed these pale people dared anything, with words.

Here then was a possibility. Magic words, perhaps? Could

I transform fear, with an incantation make anything I wished vanish, or the man who would see me appear?

I was a bit excited. And also if my words were printed, I might become important, like a singer or a dancer, but without the flaws: no need to see them staring, no need to meet the audience.

One night, instead of turning on the radio, I sat down and wrote a poem. The only one I've ever written, and I can't remember a word of it. Just that it was to do with fear, my most familiar subject. Fifteen lines of it, etched out late into a night. Like the classes, it was not as hard as I had expected, no need for rhyming or scanning. Just words poured out with a pen, becoming a poem on the paper.

I stared at the words and found they did not dissolve the fear; just made it something that could be stared at.

If I gave them away then? The next meeting of the group that put out the magazine was three weeks away: enough time to prepare for what might be my first step to twenty. I could go out and buy a black turtleneck sweater and maybe write another poem. I could go to the meeting of those people and drop fear in their laps.

I wonder if I could have. I'm curious now if I might have seen my poem in that magazine and how I would have looked in a black sweater and if I might have been some other Edna.

Instead, Harry came one day between the poem and the meeting and there was no need to long for anything again. The swan and the butterfly himself he was, not me.

And I turned twenty, and everything was changed, as I had hoped. Except that I was not changed so much; just what Harry taught me.

Little fluttering hopes of the child Edna, the lost babies of dreams.

But Harry was quite real.

I'd almost forgotten all that, from more than twenty years ago. Now those people are only dark skins and dark turtleneck sweaters in my mind.

And now my words are here, in this blue notebook. I could not manage, I guess, words and Harry, too. Or had no need to.

How mysterious it was, still is, how people laugh and talk so easily, touch and hold hands and clap each other on the back. They pick up telephones and dial the numbers and know what to say after hello. They may read aloud, or tell each other things they know, share recipes or troubles. They pour each other drinks and light each other's cigarettes and glance into each other's eyes. In my own living room, with Harry's arm around me, or even standing across the room, I have been able to do some of this also. I have spoken, asked questions, and laughed at jokes. I have nodded and nodded, listening. Harry would tell me how people said to him, "Edna's so terrific." He said they told him what a good listener I was; how kind and some said even saintly. "It's that beatific smile," he laughed, "that glazed look you get when somebody's really boring and you're trying to be nice."

People don't seem to ask for much, or to look too far.

I feel a million words inside, leaping to get out.

And what did Harry see? In what context did he say, "I love you?" Perhaps he saw a reflection. He took me in, in any case, and held me and breathed life into me as if he had rescued a drowning victim. He taught me attitudes and sufficient words, and I adopted them gratefully, if not wholly aware of doing so.

I would say Harry raised me; the way parents are said to raise their children.

Whatever would I have been without him?

There was no need to find out. Instead, I concentrated my small courage on him, my stern bone of will, and he watched and listened on my behalf.

He looked after me in more ways than he knew.

But that we reversed our duties and he became the womb, is that some reflection of my barrenness?

9

I HEARD FOOTSTEPS running up behind me and turned, startled. One never knew.

"Sorry, did I scare you?" asked the panting boy.

I cannot seem to see his final face, but that one is clear. Intense brown eyes, long narrow nose, thin lips, wide mouth, open and confident and a little breathless. Slim tan trousers, a dark-brown belt, light-blue shirt, darker blue (nylon, I think) jacket, slung back a bit to emphasize his shoulders.

Later I would see the shoulder blades, the broadness narrowing over bones, the ribs, to a waist, and from the front, hipbones guiding flesh down to that other thing I had not seen before. And have only ever seen his. "How do you know I'm any good in bed?" he used to ask, and he was laughing, but I'm not sure if he was really joking. "You've only ever been with me."

This was much later.

He was apologizing again. "I'm sorry, I was trying to catch you but I didn't mean to scare you. You're in my English class, aren't you? Restoration?"

Yes, that was right: his face was a little familiar. But as part of a crowd, a whole class. Now was different. Now he was concentrating on me as if the street and other people were not there, only the two of us existing. (That was a gift of his, making his object of the moment his only object. I have seen him turn that brilliant probing stare on others, so flattering, a magnet to confession that small device.) "I'm Harry Cormick," he was saying. "I don't know your name."

It was Edna Lanning at the time. Later Edna Cormick. Now just Edna, I suppose. Edna all alone.

"Why I wanted to talk to you, you don't miss many classes, do you? I've seen you whenever I've been there, but I've missed a few and I thought if I could maybe look at your notes I could catch up. Just tell me if you don't want me to. But I figured if anybody was up on the stuff, it'd be you."

Well, what did I look like to him, then? Some grim drudge?

He must have seen that, laughed, said, "Sorry again, I didn't mean that the way it sounded. I thought you looked like the sort who'd help a fellow out. And besides, I wanted to meet you."

Was that true? Did it start because he wanted to meet me, or because he wanted to borrow my notes?

His hand was on my shoulder; reassuring, that, and kind and companionable. And exciting in a dim way. That and his eyes and the long slim body — maleness and a sense of mischief in him.

Maybe there isn't love at first sight, but certainly there can be some kind of powerful, immediate intriguing. I'm almost sure I recognized him right away as the face that had been missing from the mirror and the pillow.

Or maybe it might have been anybody. Although I can't imagine someone else, and to even think it might have been anyone who paid attention is vicious, a murder of Harry's spirit, his distinction. Too cruel to think it might not have mattered at all.

"So can I borrow your notes?"

He must have wondered why I was silent for so long. "Yes," I said finally, then thought that sounded too abrupt, and added, "Yes, of course. But they're in my apartment." As if that were some blinding obstacle.

"Well, if you're on your way home now, I could come with you. Then," and he grinned, "if somebody else comes pounding up behind you, you won't have to be scared. I'll beat them all off."

He talked and talked, filling all the gaps. "I'm in business and it's been a bitch the last few weeks. That's why I've missed so many English classes. You in English?"

"Yes."

"First year?"

"Uh-huh."

"I've just got the one English course. I guess in business they don't figure you have to be able to talk real good." What a delightful laugh he had. It sounded as if he enjoyed himself.

"I always think we look like penguins changing classes. All those three-piece suits and white shirts. I spend half my time studying at the laundromat."

How astonishing, someone who could make fun of himself and the face he presented to the world. How brave and confident.

"What about when you graduate? What do you think you'll do?" (Show an interest, my mother's magazines had said. Show you think he is important. I paid attention, if my mother didn't.)

But I did think he was important. Or might be.

"Join some company, I guess. I'm not sure what. There'll be something. What I want, though, is power, you see."

Honest. Flat honest: that he could admit a motive so carelessly and cheerfully, and a motive not necessarily a pure or a good one, and to a stranger. "Of course I'll have to work my way up to that. I'm not patient, but you have to do that. I want to make decisions, I want to have an effect on how things work."

This did not make him a reformer, or someone who wanted to alter from within. No grand schemes here, and he was honest about that, too. No, he was happy to steer launchings of new products, make deals, and shuffle contracts, the sweet and simple authority of it all. His joy was in power, however directed. "It's almost like coming," he told me once.

He walked behind me, up the stairs to my apartment. It made me uneasy, wondering how I looked from behind.

"I'll get my notes."

"Do you have any coffee? We could have a coffee first.

Unless you have to do something. Do you have time?"

Of course. If he wanted to stay, I would make all the coffee he could drink.

"Nice place," he said, but not enthusiastically. I looked around and saw it for the first time as an outsider would have to. No one had been here before but me, and my father that first day.

Yes, it was shabby. The house itself was shabby, the hallway and the stairs were shabby, and so was this apartment on the second floor. But it was mine.

After all these years of comfortable middle-classness, even I remember it with some dismay; if also recollected fondness. After so many years of tables suiting chairs, and couches and curtains matching, that apartment would be unthinkable now. But it was mine.

This room, where I sit so straight by the large window, is not mine. It was not my choice, and has nothing to do with me. Only that first apartment and then the house were mine.

It was not, I think, because that apartment was so shabby that I didn't have the same compulsion to keep it spotless that I did later with the house. I think it was because just for me, that wasn't so important. In my house, for Harry, it was vital.

The apartment had a small single bed behind a heavy curtain that hung by rings from a bar across the doorway separating the tiny corner that was the bedroom from the living room. There, a cot with green, brown, and yellow cushions, ghastly now in memory, was the couch. A heap of books was piled against a wall. Later Harry made me a bookcase from red bricks and golden boards, the kind he said a lot of students had.

The kitchen had a battered fridge and stove, a small counter, single sink, and two rough cupboards, two chipped cream-painted wooden kitchen chairs, and an old, small wooden table for both studying and eating. Beyond it was the bathroom, with old and irrevocably stained fixtures. I had scrubbed and scrubbed them, with the thought that the stains were who knew what kind of germs, but it made no difference.

When I think of that apartment now, I have an impression of length and darkness, an aura of past tenants' grime and cooking odours and paleness and unhealth, and my own small efforts to overcome all that. But then, it was mine.

I made the coffee while he looked around. "Why this?" he asked, and he was pointing to a wall in the living room.

Well, I had made some attempts to decorate with things that struck me, colour photographs clipped from magazines and pinned unframed to the walls. The one he was pointing to was a portrait of a young girl dancing, whirling, entirely intent on herself, her movements, and her body.

"Oh her," I said. What could I say about what she meant? "It makes me feel good to look at her, she seems so happy and full of what she's doing." This was true: some uplifting about her concentrated joy.

"And this one?"

This was an old woman full of lines and thought.

"Well, I think that's character. She's suffered, you see, in her life, and it's like she's saying, 'It can be tough but I've gotten something from it. I made it.' She's — triumphant, kind of." That did not properly explain what I saw in the lines of that old woman's face, but part of it.

Did he hear my fear? Or maybe he thought I was profound, or sensitive. He sipped at his too-bitter coffee, asked, "You like living alone?"

"Oh yes." I had no idea. It was simply how it was.

Did he, from that, deduce that I was independent and certain of myself? Certainly he could not have seen me as I saw myself, and I was careful that he shouldn't.

"Maybe," he said at last, "I could take a look at those notes."

Of course he would want to do that, he'd want to go over them quickly and leave. I know what it means, that expression, "My heart sank." That's precisely what it was, the heart sinking like a stone.

The apartment wouldn't be the same when he was gone. As if he'd been a breeze and a light flowing through the place, all its bits of nastiness had been exposed. When he left, I would be lonely instead of just alone.

All this because he had the missing face. Because he laughed and spoke the truth and because his body was lean and because he was here, in my apartment.

"You have really clear handwriting," he was saying. "How do you do that when you have to go so fast in class?"

"Oh, I just take things down in point form. I write up the real notes later." And then could have kicked myself: appearing once more the drudge. I might as well have greasy hair and glasses.

"Must take a lot of time."

He was standing, leaving, and I would see him out the door and down the stairs and gone and that would be the end of it. How would I be able to go back into that apartment, sit down behind those curtains in my chair to watch again?

"Feel like a movie some time next week?"

The heart leaps back and floats into the throat. "Yes. Yes, I'd like that."

"Good. I'll call you in a couple of days."

"He won't," I thought. But he did.

My handwriting here, following the straight lines of this notebook, is so fine I could weep at the beauty of it.

10

LISTEN, PEOPLE INVEST IN THE STOCKMARKET, in real estate, in gold. They put their money, what is valuable to them, into something from which they believe they can expect a reasonable return. They give up, perhaps, immediate rewards for the prospect of something better in the future.

People make investments all the time. I, too. I took the only thing I had, my sole possession, myself, whatever that might have turned out to be, and invested it in Harry. People make investments all the time. Why not me?

I thought it built up, like a savings account, a safe six, eight, ten per cent a year. After a few dabblings in the market — those high school dances, the gritting of teeth, the money spent on lipsticks and powders, the university tuition, and a poem — comes the real plunge: all my assets diving into Harry.

My mother used to say, "Whatever you do will come back to you." When I was a child, that filled me with terror. My small sins — to have, in a moment of wanton rebellion, stuck out my tongue at her behind her back; to have secretly plucked all the hair from one of Stella's dolls; to have ridden my bicycle around the block when I was not supposed to go beyond the corner — these things made the night uneasy. I wondered what form my sins might take, returning on me.

But it should work the other way as well. If I did good, kind, and helpful things, they should also come back to me.

I was as good as it seemed reasonable to be. I am no

saint, and one has to make accommodations to reality. Otherwise there would be nothing one could eat that did not have some wickedness in its past, and no place one could move (although I didn't move a great deal, and for myself, ate little).

I was faithful and tried to be kind. When people came to the door canvassing for heart funds or for cancer, I gave them dollar bills. And I read the newspapers and magazines, I could identify the worst offenders, and if I saw grapes in the supermarket that came from Chile, or apples from South Africa, I did not buy them if there was some other choice.

But one must have a sense of balance about these things. Harry liked grapes (as I did, for that matter), and he also liked crisp, sharp-tasting apples. Those places were so far away, and Harry was right here. And there were conflicting viewpoints: what difference did it make if I did not buy the grapes? Who was hurt? The generals in Chile would not say, "Edna Cormick didn't buy our food today," and in South Africa they did not say, "Edna Cormick turned down our apples." Of course I believed in peace and full stomachs and in fairness. (It's only fair, Edna, said Dottie Franklin.) But who or what was I intended to serve first? The man who came home, or faceless people far away?

I was not the sort of person to carry a sign, march in front of an embassy, shout slogans into television cameras. I was a small woman doing her best. These things are too big for such a person to work out, and all I could do was my best; so I tried to keep my own small portion safe and pass by the grapes and apples when there was some other choice, and thought if I made my own tiny universe safe and good, that should be enough, and would meet the payments on whatever might be owed.

Maybe I didn't go far enough. But I went further than a lot of other people. And I was unobtrusive. Who would notice me, going down a street or in a supermarket aisle?

For such a failure in my investment, I should have been another person altogether.

I invested the goodness I had in Harry, and I did expect compounded goodness would be my return.

A blue-chip stock, my life with Harry should have been.

11

"TALK TO ME, EDNA," he'd say.

Yes, but what about?

Really, I preferred to listen. And really, he preferred to talk. He'd given up quite a lot for me, I thought — other girls, for instance, there'd been those — and there weren't so many ways I could repay him for that. Listening, mainly. All I gave up was writing out my notes each evening and my watching. Maybe poems. But poems vanished when he appeared. If they had ever come, it would have been from fear and desolation, and Harry filled so much space that fear and desolation sank deeper and deeper under his weight until they were just small things crouching at the bottom of my soul.

Even the dancing and singing life was gone. No time for it now, and who needed made-up things when real events were going on?

We went to movies or to bars (where I found that beer has a queer and bitter taste and wondered how people, including Harry, could enjoy so much of it), and often we sat in my living room. It was private there, just the two of us. We couldn't often go to his apartment because he shared it with another business student and it was hard to be alone.

He'd sit beside me on the cot-couch, hands folded behind his head, eyes closed, telling dreams. "I want so many things, Edna," he said. "To do something big. It's not just being rich, although," and he laughed, "that's part of it, that would be nice. But it's doing something, making something, being somebody. I don't want to get old and die and think I missed anything or that nobody noticed me or it didn't matter. I want to matter."

I nodded, although his eyes were closed. "Yes, I know." Although in fact I didn't. He seemed to see much further than I. My own vision now didn't go beyond his closed-eyed presence in my living room, where I could lean forward and touch him.

But whether I understood or not was not the point. The point was, he trusted me with his dreams. "You'll be somebody," I told him.

If he had gotten old, would he have been satisfied? Would he have been able to sit back and say, "Yes, I missed nothing. People noticed. What I did mattered. I mattered"?

"Talk to me, Edna," he said sometimes.

"What about?"

"You. I've told you what I want, now it's your turn. Tell me what you want."

I wanted him; but that was too bold a thing to say.

"I'm not sure. I'm not like you, I'm not sure what I want."

"But you must have some ideas, some plans. For what you'll do when you graduate."

"Well, there's only so much you can do with a degree in English. I'll probably end up teaching." Dreary prospect; one reason I didn't care to look beyond the slim figure unwound in my living room, whose presence astonished me and seemed a miracle, which I couldn't tell him because it would say far too much about the fear.

"And get married some day?" His eyes were glinting, laughing: testing my intent to trap him?

"Maybe. If it happens."

"But you're not really aiming at anything in particular? There's nothing you have in mind that you really want to do?"

He made me feel very small and useless. Amazed, he was, that someone young and starting out would not have a dream. I could have said, perhaps, "I've thought of telling stories, or seeing Timbuktu." But those were only fantasies.

"Okay then," he was saying, "if there's nothing special you want to do, what do you want to be?"

There was a difference? I frowned and shook my head. I might have said, "I want to be safe," or "I want to be happy," but that would have disappointed him, and sounded stupid even unspoken and I didn't want to answer stupidly, so kept silent.

I do see now, though, what he might have meant. I spent all those years with him assuming that I was what I was doing and that I was doing what I was. But now I've done something that must be different from what I am, I cannot be a person who would do that. So maybe that's sort of what he meant. Although nothing so drastic, I'm sure.

"You want kids?"

"Well yes, I suppose so." It was not a matter of longing for children, no maternal yearnings and growlings deep in my body somewhere; only an assumption. Children appeared in people's lives, the order of things, and I supposed that in the order of things they would appear in mine. What was inconceivable, although becoming less so with Harry in my living room when he could have been other places, was the gap between who I was and getting there.

"I can see you as a mother. You'd be a good one."

Possibly that was true.

Other nights, other questions. "Tell me about your family," he demanded, and I did what I could.

"It doesn't sound to me as if you like them much."

"But of course I love them." Startled. "They're my family."

"Maybe. But it doesn't sound as though you like them."

He tried to make me see these differences: between being and doing, liking and loving. He was much wiser than I.

He always seemed to see things more clearly. He wasn't afraid. Except once, he was afraid.

His eyes were open and he was looking at me. "You don't like talking about yourself, do you? You're shy."

It was the kindness, the rare gentleness on his face, the care, that did it.

"I don't know how."

That just came blurting out, and the words hung there all by themselves. It shook me, hearing the echoes of them. There was some great rock lodged in my chest that had been there as long as I could remember, so that I had taken its weight for granted, and all of a sudden it was breaking into splinters and pieces were flying loose and the weight was gone and I was trembling, my face was all screwing up on itself and tears were pouring down it, out of my control.

"Hey!" He must have been astounded. "What's the matter? Edna? What is it?" His arms were around me, a hand was pressing my face into his shoulder and he was rocking me back and forth, back and forth, crooning, "Hey, hey, it's all right," a lullaby, letting me weep.

Oh, sometimes I had cried — as a child for hurt knees, in my teens for loneliness — but never before like this, not with my whole body wrenching like some kind of fit, tears flushing all my veins and arteries. It hurt, and I wanted to stop; but also didn't want to, the rocking and crooning were pleasant and comforting and kept me safe while I cried. It went on and on while I thought, "Oh God, it's so awful," by which I meant everything, I think, up till then, and also, "This is so nice." It made it hard to stop, but finally the tears hit bone and finished, and I felt limp and weary and was hiccuping as well. I thought, "I must really trust him to be able to do this." And then thought, "So I must really love him." I'd only permitted that word in fantasy before, made-up conversations, drifting off to sleep alone.

I straightened, wiped my face. "I'm sorry," I said, "I must look awful." I didn't want him to see me ugly, now that I was alert to love right here in the flesh. One of the things I understood was looking one's best in order to get love in return.

"You look fine." He was stroking my hair, and down along my shoulder and my arm. His voice was so gentle. If mine was shaken, his was kind.

I think now that if he had never seen me weep, we never

might have married. I think it made that difference.

Later, I could say to him, without a tremor or a hint of tears, "You know, I've never heard anybody in my family say, 'I love you.' Nobody has ever said it." I now found that strange, although it hadn't occurred to me quite that way before. Now I could see because I was away and because Harry was teaching me to see and because I could trust and therefore love him.

"Well then, why don't you say it? Maybe it only takes one person and you'd shake things up so everybody could."

But it would be like walking naked in front of them. Everything might disintegrate with the shock.

His people, when I eventually met them, were quite different. His mother was small and grey-haired and charming and his father was big and tall and grey-haired and courtly. They touched each other often and smiled at Harry. Just small touches, a pat on the hand or the back. They seemed fond of each other, and they were proud of Harry. He was their only child. "That makes a difference," he said. "They only had me to love."

Yes, well that hurt a bit, although he wouldn't have meant it to.

They were well-dressed and prosperous. His mother wore a grey silk dress that made her hair glint at the lunch at which Harry introduced us all, and his father wore a charcoal three-piece suit. Harry, too. "It's the family uniform," he joked.

I wore a new dress that Harry had helped me choose. I had only ordinary school clothes, skirts and sweaters. This dress was cotton, ivory with thin pink stripes. Plain, with matched buttons down the front and a matching belt around the waist. Simple, and a bit expensive. Another thing I was learning: that simplicity can cost more than the elaborate, and is in better taste.

I also bought white pumps and a small white handbag for the occasion.

They were pleasant and polite and kind and proper. Prosperous, although not rich, and their prosperity and satisfaction showed in small ways that made them different from my family — the way they handled their forks, the way they ate — the meal a ceremony of some pleasure, not an uncomfortable tongue-tying necessity. I managed to say some things about myself and to ask polite questions in return. Harry carried things along. It seemed he could take care of any awkward moments. Afterward he said they liked me. "They said you seem a nice girl," and he grinned as if we knew much better. It was a new pleasure to be secretly daring, cleverly deceptive; because by then we were going to bed together, an astonishing leap for someone like me so many years ago.

I wonder what they would have thought of me if they had known? I wonder how I felt myself?

Our two families at the wedding, such a contrast. Except for Stella, of course, who danced and danced and seemed more likely to be Harry's sister than mine.

12

HE HAD A WONDERFUL BODY.

"Edna, come on," he said. "I love you." I could never, despite my joy and greed for him, have been the first to say those words. But now he demanded, "You love me, don't you?" It was hard: as if the words were taboo, and I could be struck down for saying them.

True enough, one can be. They leave quite a gap.

I thought myself a moral person, and this was more than twenty years ago, when these things mattered. But Harry's and mine was a separate world, a small and enclosed universe, and nothing outside seemed to apply here.

He undressed me slowly, gently, and with admiration in each step. He kissed each breast and then, startlingly, my thighs. He was — almost pure about it; as if he were removing wrappings from a lovely statue. As if the object were to worship, not to hold.

But he did hold. I lay beneath blankets while he undressed. He was much quicker with himself than with me: swift, efficient undoing of buttons, a shrug to discard the shirt, a zipper rasp, hands thrust beneath elastic, bending, stepping free, sitting on the end of the bed, leaning over for the socks and then standing and this was it, a naked man.

I thought of mirrors and pillows and what had been unimaginable then and would now be real.

He slid beneath the blankets with me, turned on his side. For a while he just touched fingers and lips lightly here and there. I felt, now and then, tremors rippling through his body, but he was patient.

This was pleasant. It really did feel fine, as I'd imagined, to feel the length of a body, warm all the way down, along-side mine.

I was nervous when he pulled the covers back and raised himself up on one elbow to stare at me; but I was proud, too, that my body did not have obvious flaws. His did not either, although I could see his bones. It was fine and hard and slim.

He never let his body go. Neither of us let ourselves get flabby.

The act itself wasn't long enough for me to absorb all the things it meant. That here he was, this man, this real warm flesh, this piece of magic. I was too amazed to be very aware of the thing itself.

But we did it again and again. There was plenty of time. There were hours in that little bed. It remained a miracle, to have this body everywhere around me.

Afterward, when he collapsed, his face in my neck and the length of him a warm weight along the length of me, that was the time I liked best: when I could stroke his shoulders and his hair, tenderness and gentleness in my own hands, repaying his before. That was my time, afterward.

We slept curled together. Nothing could reach me, with his body wrapped behind mine, a long arm flung over my ribs, across my breasts.

It wasn't the way one reads about, all that ecstasy in novels. I guess that was somehow what I'd been expecting, but it wasn't that way at all. I thought it was probably better, in a way, to feel the warmth and tenderness, if not the passion.

He felt the passion, I'm sure that was unmistakable. And it made me a bit uneasy. It seemed wrong for him to need me so much, to show so much desire, when the truth, apart from bodies, was the opposite.

I prefer to give than to receive; to need than to be needed; to want than to be wanted. The pressure of being given to, wanted, needed, is hard for me.

When I was a girl kissing pillows and mirrors, I thought, "Well, this is practice. It will be different with the real thing."

Of course it was different. Pillows and mirrors do not kiss breasts or hold you in the night.

But I'd thought the difference would be something else: that in the act there would be a loss of self, a splitting of bonds. I thought when it happened I would soar beyond myself to some place unaware and free. That I might disappear completely. I'd imagined some transcendence that would be unimaginable and indescribable.

I was amazed by the kind of magic there was in that small bed with Harry; but also amazed that the other magic, apparently, was an illusion.

Because all the time, each time, before and while he was inside and afterward, there I was, my body and all my thoughts, alert to each sensation and every move, all the pantings and perspiration. Not for a moment was I lost.

Are there people who get lost? Or do the books lie, as they seem to have about so many other things?

But I was safe.

I was safe even in ways I hadn't considered. I must have assumed that if outside rules did not apply in our two-person world, outside accidents would also not occur.

Harry was not so foolish. He must have been looking at it all quite differently from me, and it's just as well, although ironic that it turned out to be unnecessary.

There were strange shufflings and cracklings, clumsy shiftings, but I didn't catch on right away what he was doing. Afterward, there was a small damp milky balloon twisted shut with a knot, lying beside the bed.

It was repulsive, a white slug of a thing, and Harry caught my surprised grimace. "It's a safe, honey," he said, and leaning over me, picked it up. "So you don't get pregnant. See all those little maybe-babies? Zillions of the little devils."

Later he told me he didn't like using them. "You don't feel as much as you do without them." So what did he feel? So much pumping and desire with them, how much without?

Such a puzzle to understand someone else's body. Oh, I

could *watch* his, he encouraged me to look at him and even touch him, and I got used to the sight of him rising and flushing and the feeling of him jerking and throbbing to the touch of my fingertips; and later I could see him shrinking, fading, and withdrawing. But how it happened, that was some excitement I could not grasp.

He tried to watch me in the same way, but I wouldn't let him. Those parts, I think, are not beautiful. Those parts of him weren't beautiful either, but he was so proud. He looked at himself sometimes with wonder, as if he also didn't understand it. It must be odd to be a man, so exposed. In women, everything is tucked away and hidden.

So I didn't understand his body, no. But I thought the act in general was of the heart, not of the body, and that those parts of us down there were symbols, ways of showing, and not the thing itself.

"I love you," we told each other before and after. During, even he was mute.

13

AND THEN THERE WE WERE, married, and there I was safe on the other side of twenty and the gap. A leap hand in hand with Harry, like in a movie.

Twenty years between then and the appearance of another gap and a leap into danger again. Still, twenty years of safety.

What if he hadn't asked? But I was sure he would.

I was sure he had to. From the first moment, his presence, his existence, blocked the world. I could not see it, nor could it touch me. He surrounded me, was in every direction I looked, filling up my view.

Once we went to a public beach and, far out in the water, standing up and moving with the waves, made love. It must have been apparent, if anyone had looked, what we were doing; and I never thought of that. Or if I did, it was only that a watcher would be far off and anonymous, while here was Harry. We were invisible, or our passion must have blinded people. We were all that existed, our twined-together two-ness made all the world our own possession, unreal except as we might admit it. It was delicious, this satisfying protection we made together.

Did I fill up his view that way? I suppose I didn't. He may have been keeping an eye on the beach over my shoulder.

What if he hadn't asked? If I'd gone out and found a job, taught English all these years, hating it I'm sure, putting my own pay cheques in the bank, paying rent on some small apartment somewhere, watching, watching all the time all the ordinary people, coveting their ordinariness — would

I choose that if I could undo how this has ended?

I had twenty years. I can't see giving them up. The thing is to see how much was true.

He was quite a while working up to asking. Sometimes I saw him watching me in a speculative way, and I thought I knew what he was wondering. I did my best; was my best. And finally, I guess, he too found it the only thing to be done, came to my conclusion (but by what route?), took a deep breath, said, "Let's get married."

He sat beside me on my old couch-cot, holding both my hands, turned towards me, looking at me, more than that, into me — was he trying to see through and past me into the future, to calculate the risk?

"But before you answer," he was saying, "we have to have an understanding." I nodded willingly. Whatever.

"The thing is, I'm scared of feeling trapped. I know myself, and I know I can't take that feeling. So if we're going to do the paper and promises, I want to be sure they won't make any difference. I know you let me be, but sometimes that can change when people get married, and I have to be able to feel free. I don't want to have to answer to anybody."

"But," I protested, "have I ever?"

No, I was careful. I said, "Don't worry about it, that's fine," when he called to say he had to study or was going out for a drink with some friends. I would never have said, "Oh, but I was counting on you. I have nothing else to do."

"No, of course you haven't, or we wouldn't still be together. Look, I'll tell you what I think: if I had to feel responsible I'd resent it, and when I resent something I get mad and then I blow up and get the hell away from whatever it is. See?

"But if I don't feel any demands, I can give you everything. I'll want to give you everything. It's just a matter of whether I feel forced or not. I have to want to want to.

"Do you see what I mean at all? I know I'm putting it badly. I didn't mean to, I had it all worked out how to say it, but I got off the track," and he gave me that appealing, tippy little smile he had, where one side of his mouth went up and the skin around his eyes wrinkled around them, so that he was kind of peeking, like a little boy.

Well yes, I could see in a way what he meant, looking at it from his point of view and knowing him as I did.

Me, I was the opposite. I longed for the obligations and the demands. They would fence my life.

One would think that would make us fit perfectly together. It did seem to.

Still, I was a little hurt that he could apparently foresee me so easily as a burden. On the other hand, he was honest at least. "But I love you," I said, as if that would explain everything.

"I love you, too," he said and smiled and leaned forward and kissed my forehead.

When we made love, I could feel the perfect infinite future of this. It made it a much larger event.

I never broke the promise. Whatever else, I never broke that promise. It hardly even seemed to matter that I had made it. He told me so much: it didn't seem possible there could be any secrets.

He broke it. I never did.

In those days, one pledged to "love, honour, and obey," although I gather that has now changed and one can promise what one wants. Or not. Sometimes it seems no one promises anything any more.

But I took the pledge for granted; welcomed it, in fact.

What about him? Was he frightened, despite our private pact, of love, honour, and obedience? Did he look at me uneasily and wonder what he might be giving up?

I was uneasy and afraid. I was afraid I might not be good enough, that my alertness might falter for a moment, and like a broken spell, all this would vanish.

I felt I was being called to perfection (and it was just like that, a vocation, something one is called to — by whom? what?) and I might not measure up. I added more private, silent promises: to be indispensable and absolute.

Obviously I failed. Obviously there were things missed, the small pin lodged in the carpet. I did not try quite hard enough, although I did try very hard.

I'm sure I could have been perfect, with more effort. And then Harry might have been perfect too. As it was, there were flaws and shortcomings, and his faults, although more glaring and gashing, were only reflections of my own.

"Ah, you're perfect, Edna," he told me sometimes. But I was not.

So much hung on that day we were married: all my unhappy, forlorn past and all our brilliant, sturdy future. There would have had to be great fireworks, explosions in the sky, and rumblings and upheavals in the earth, to be the day it meant to me.

Of course there were not. But I was dazed by expectations. They were: that marrying Harry resolved — everything. I would work hard at it, true, but it was work I could understand and could do and that had a purpose. I was safe, inside two, and questions and fear had no place any more; might even be a kind of wickedness, betrayal. That is what twenty years meant, although at the time I pictured it forever.

So much fussing, and none to do with the point of all this. Stella pushing and pulling at my hair, my mother tugging at my dress. They worried about the flowers for the church and whether the guests would all be seated properly. They went over the order of people in the receiving line, and were nervous when the photographer was late. But it was all for me, they were on my side: they too wanted this to be perfect.

I would have liked to stop. To sit alone for a while in my bedroom and let what it meant soak into me, to absorb it until I could feel it fill me.

But there was no time, and no quiet.

"If I can remember everything," I thought, "I'll be able to go over it later as much as I want." But while I could, and did many times, the recollection was as unreal as the reality.

To be married, wasn't that something, now. I couldn't even look at Harry in the ceremony. He would have to be enormous, fill up the church to its gilded rafters, to be what he meant.

I overheard my mother saying, "Isn't it nice to see Edna so happy and relaxed." I was frantic with excitement, which may have been similar to happiness. But I was certainly not relaxed. This was my life here, didn't she see?

I heard Harry's voice beside me in the ceremony and felt his hand on my elbow as we walked back up the aisle. His arm rested alongside mine in the receiving line, and at the reception I heard him laughing and talking beside me, and felt him pulling me to my feet when they tinkled the glasses for a kiss. We were our own magic circle in the midst of all this, but I closed my eyes.

I lay awake that night listening to my husband breathe beside me. I'd lain awake before, listening to Harry breathe, but this was new: Harry my husband, my husband Harry.

It seems to me that what he was saying that day was, "In return for this, I get that." And what I was saying was, "In return for this, I will always have that."

14

WHAT DID HE SEE? What did he see all those years?

Oh God, I want to know. I want him here. I want to talk to him and ask him, I want him to tell me what it was all about and what he saw. I want to know why.

It must have been quite different from my view. That's what's shattering, how different it must have been.

If we could talk now, we could tell the truth.

I guess I miss Harry. I suppose I mourn him in a way. Although I can't quite grasp it.

But what I do miss is his presence. We could sit and chat, I miss that, just the sound of his voice, even a conversation about what to watch on television, even that I would cherish. We could sit on the couch together, him with a newspaper or a magazine, me with a book. The quietness. I took the ordinary quietness for granted. I would like to see him reach forward to pour another glass of wine, or to light my cigarette. I would like to be out in the car with him, hear him cursing another driver or singing with the radio. I'd like to hear him arguing with one of the men from his office. I'd like to hear him say, "Another drink, Don? How about you, Lois?" when we had company. I would like to see him gulping orange juice in the morning, saying, "Jesus Christ, I'm late." I would like to hear his car in the driveway, the garage door opening and closing, his "Hi, Edna, God what a day, feel like a drink?" I would like to feel his hand touch my shoulder lightly or see him grin as he grabbed my breasts or pinched my bottom as he passed by me. I would like once again to lie awake in the night listening to him breathe. I would like to be wakened by a snore. I would like to be cleaning the bathroom in the morning and smell his aftershave, and to fold his pyjamas beneath his pillow. I would like to pull the covers off our vacant bed and see the imprint of his body, both our bodies, and know they would be there again. I would like to empty the ashtray, filled with the butts of our cigarettes. Where did it all go? I would like to reach back and have it all again.

15

THEY SAY IT'S NEARLY the middle of October. What good are pages and pages of neat, precise letters spiralling into tidy words and paragraphs, if they only look good? Underneath it is a mess.

I must look more closely, pay more attention, see everything. All the details and the tiny things, that must be where it is.

So I note, sitting here in this flowered chair, notebook squarely in my lap, my back rigid against the cushioned softness, that some leaves are falling.

The ones that fall are darker than the others and seem to be more crinkled at the edges. Far away are the pine trees, but these closer ones are maples, shades of green, red, yellow, and orange, some brown, all melting through the limbs.

If I watch carefully from day to day, and this is the sort of concentration that is required, I should be able to see a single leaf altering: the green fading to the other colours and then the winding and twisting to the earth. First small yellow blotches, then one of the deeper colours; or for some, merely a swift passage to dull brown. The veins turn dark. When the bright colours begin to turn dull, the stems weaken and the leaves lose their grip. Today it is windy, and many of them are falling, some perhaps prematurely, because of the wind. On the ground it doesn't take long until they're dry and flaky.

There is one there, holding on, almost a perfect deep red, easy to spot. The branch it's on is whipping in the wind, and most of the other leaves around it have already given up and gone. This one tosses, but does not let go.

The brilliant red leaf struggles stubbornly and dumbly. Can a small leaf beat the wind? It sways and curls upward with the force, straining at its frail connection to the branch, the trunk, the roots.

A small leaf cannot beat the wind. A stronger gust catches at its weakest point, there is a last tug, and it is drifting, drifting away and down, resting gently in a perfect landing on the ground. Now it's hard to pick out, skiffled a little by the breeze so that it dances as if it were still alive. In another shuffling, it disappears among all the others.

A man goes out, carrying a rake. A foolish day for such a job. He should wait until the wind dies down. I would like to rap on the window and draw his attention to the mistake.

I suppose, though, he's been told to do it. Here, routines, schedules, and orders are important, if not always sensible. I can see it has to be that way.

In any case he doesn't appear to care. His raking is perfunctory and listless, unseeing. He doesn't even try to capture all the leaves for his piles beneath the trees, just drags his rake along the surface and doesn't go back for those uncaught. How can he be satisfied with such a job? He walks away, rake over his shoulder, while behind him the wind tosses at his work, busily undoing it. He will have to do it all again tomorrow.

If I had his job I would find every leaf and put it in the pile, and I would put them all neatly into some container so they couldn't blow away. It's so simple, so apparent. He should be grateful to have a job that requires him to do only a simple apparent task perfectly. He should be happy to do it properly. So many mistakes that man must make.

Although he is not unusual, I see here many things not done right. Sometimes it seems to me that people see only circles: their jobs are done in circles, and corners are always missed.

The woman who vacuums in this room, for instance,

never gets right into the corners, and when she washes the windows or the mirrors, she makes only circles on the glass, misses the square edges. There are always smudges in the corners. No wonder there are bits of dust and straight pins in the carpets. Am I the only one who sees? The only one who knows the importance of the unlikely, hidden spots? These people do the same things again and again, and they never do them absolutely.

Maybe they think it doesn't matter, because it all has to be done again.

I could tell them. I would say, "Look, I kept a house for years and it was spotless." (But then, obviously it was not quite spotless: some corner missed.) But I could tell them anyway that it doesn't matter that the dishes will have to be done again and the floors and windows washed again. It doesn't matter. It must all be done properly, exactly, each and every time. Some pollution, a taint, will get a grip otherwise.

You have to take some care. And you need pride, too, some pride in your work.

I know it doesn't *look* important. I know there are people who might say I wasted time (twenty years?) and that my work was menial, unskilled, unpaid, excessive.

The jobs themselves were, this is true enough. But the people who might say my work was small, they wouldn't be seeing beyond to what it added up to: all those little jobs, they were my payment and my expression of my duty and my care. They added up to safety and escape, love and gratitude spoken in a different language, words in shining floors and tidy beds. There is nothing menial or unskilled about that.

And if Harry might not always notice all that was done, he would certainly have noticed if it hadn't been. Sometimes if we'd been out to dinner at the home of some man he worked with, he'd say things that demonstrated that. "I've never seen fresh flowers in that house," he said. Or "Christ, frozen cake for dessert, that's really shitty." Or "Jesus, crap piled all over the place in that house, how can Dave put up with it? Magazines and toys, it would take her two minutes to pick that stuff up. And the glasses weren't even really clean."

And then he might say, "Oh, I know she works, she probably gets too tired. I'm glad you don't have to. I'm glad you're free."

Free? Did he say that? A curious kind of freedom, to clean and cook. I don't suppose he thought it easy, but did he really think it free? But what would I have done with freedom anyway?

I had strict rules, things I did not permit myself. I didn't let myself say, "I'm tired, let's just stay home." I never said, "I think I'll just let the dishes go tonight," or "You'll have to wear the blue shirt, all the rest are in the wash." I kept on top of things and was agreeable to suggestions. When he came home he found ease and choices. I did not mean to open up so many choices, though. If he thought me free, did he think he should be also?

That leaf I was watching, it's just one of a thousand now. Much good it did it, putting up a fight.

One thing to watch; another, the next step in the pursuit of detail, to touch and examine closely. I am not allowed to go outside. So I ask a nurse, "Will you bring me a leaf? Next time you're coming in, could you pick one up for me?" She is startled, because I hardly ever speak.

I am amazed and touched that she remembers.

If I had chosen, it would have been a vivid leaf, still orange or yellow. This one is already mainly brown and beginning to crinkle. I see that the nurse's caring, like everything else, is imperfect. It would have taken such a small effort, an extra step, to find a beauty for me.

Still, it's something. This is not my own life any more, and I don't get to choose.

Ah, but it falls apart so quickly. I stroke its veins and crumbling bits fall off. I touch its dryness and it disintegrates. Small pieces, turning into dust. The cleaning woman vacuums but does not get all the dust, and it digs more deeply into the floor, grinding in.

If a leaf, perhaps a flower? (Is it necessary to want more and more, to go further and further?) I ask the nurse and she's a bit annoyed, I see a quick frown and I can hear her think, "What next?" Again a care with limits, imperfections.

I would like to see colour and grace. She brings two late roses, thorns snipped off (to prevent accidental pain, or because she thinks I might deliberately hurt myself?). They are full and pale and pink and wilting at the edges. "I'm sorry they're past their best," she says. "But I thought you might as well have them. They're from the border around the front." There are flowers here? I must have passed them coming in, but I didn't see. It must be a long time ago.

The leaves on the rose stems are bright harsh green, the petals soft and smooth and slinky. The stems themselves are tough and wounded, scarred where the thorns have been snipped away. The flowers are dying.

One by one the petals drop off and the water in the glass in which the nurse has put the roses turns musky. Each petal is velvet. Each drops to the floor.

In the end there are just ragged brown stumps on limp stems. The cleaning woman says, "Look, these are dead now," and puts them in the garbage, pouring the dregs of the water down the sink. I hear a tap turned on and water running, flushing it all away. "Such a mess, all these bits and pieces," she complains, stooping to retrieve the dead petals and leaves from the floor.

Was I ever impatient with my work? Sometimes, it's true, I didn't feel like doing it. But I always did it. Putting it off might well become a degenerating process; like having a solitary drink in the afternoon, it might turn into something huge. Alcoholism; or sloth. It only takes one slip.

"Doesn't anything make you angry?" Harry asked me sometimes. Puzzled because his own temper was quick. It was also, though, swift to finish.

"Why be angry?" I asked him. "What's there to be angry at?"

His anger came and flared and was gone. Mine, I think, if I had felt it, would have been quite real and deep. And maybe like the drink in the afternoon or the job deferred. I chose, instead, floors and windows.

I could say to Harry again now, "What is there to be angry at? What is worth anger?"

I can't even summon anger that so many things, leaves and flowers, are disappearing, and that there's nothing I can do to stop or change it. I would like to, but I am not angry at the impossibility. I am, however, a little sad.

16

FOR WEEKS AFTER WE WERE MARRIED, I woke in the mornings and turned to watch Harry sleeping and, remembering with wonder, thought, "I'm married." It remained a miracle, and a mystery how I could have landed safely here in this soft bed.

It was not only a miracle, but a conclusion. I'd longed for the normal, the ordinary, and now here was my life, normal and ordinary. No more freakish standing aside, watching the others with their secret. I'd found the man, or been found, which was how things ought to be; and we were married, which was how things ought to be; and now I could go about performing this life the way it was supposed to be performed. It was like having the pattern of a dress to sew, merely a matter of taking something already laid out and cutting and stitching it properly, following the lines.

Being here is something like that, although it lacks the joy. It is also mainly a matter of certain things having to be done. There is a time for this, another time for that, they come and tell me just which time it is, and I do the thing, no need for decision. It has its virtues, being here.

But then there is missing, of course, the purpose. No one coming home to be the point of it.

Odd, not to weep for the loss of joy and purpose. I've cried at the oddest, most remote things and yet for Harry I haven't yet managed a proper tear.

Buckets of them in the movies of my tender-hearted childhood: for a mistreated horse, or the reunion of a boy and his lost dog. Later, a tug of moisture for a tender story in a magazine; and television shows have a way of twisting little wrinkles into the ending of even a comedy. I have found, in my evenings alone before the television set, a tear springing to the eye, trailing down a cheek.

Now is when I should be weeping. And now the ducts are dry, frozen, blocked.

"I can see you as a mother," he said to me once. "You'd be a good one." And that's another thing I've never wept for.

Because other things as well are dry, frozen, blocked.

We were married a couple of years, Harry was doing well, and we were settled in our house. I felt suited to this life in which certain things were done; I liked the view from the inside looking out.

"I think," he said one night, "it might be time to throw away the safes." Looked at me questioningly. "What do you think?"

Well yes, it might be time to move on to the next thing. This was part of it, of course.

"A boy, I think," he was grinning. "I'd like to order a boy first, if you don't mind."

A baby is what I would have liked. Just a baby. We would walk out in the sunshine, up the street and back, baby in carriage, stroller, bundled up. People would say, "Isn't he sweet?" or she, and I would smile.

To have Harry and a baby, that would be everything.

Oh, diapers too, and strange smells in the house and waking in the night. Harder, more demanding work. But to hold a baby. To be depended on for life. To actually make something out of myself.

A baby I could hold for hours; as long as I wanted, we could be close. I really hadn't seen it clearly and perfectly before, but now that it could be true, there was a great longing to hold. My arms, which had seemed full of Harry, suddenly felt too light and empty, missing a weight like an amputation.

Is it odd to be so capable of instant longings?

"First thing," and he grinned again, "we'll go out this weekend and buy a rocking chair."

Then "No, the first thing to do is throw out the safes."
He took my hand and we walked, laughing, upstairs and
he took the little package from the drawer of the bedside
table, looked inside. "Two left. Too bad to waste them." He
pulled one out, unrolled it, handed it to me. "Here, blow it
up. Like a balloon." He kept the other one himself.

They were like balloons; except a different, heavier, slip-
perier texture. Almost obscene; like the night after a party
when Harry'd had too much to drink and when we came
home, he wanted me to put my mouth on him. "Just kiss
it," he urged, but I couldn't. I just couldn't. This was something like that, but at least it was possible. And Harry thought
it was fun, was gleefully blowing up his safe and knotting
it, pinging it heavily into the air and taking mine and knotting it so that there were two of the overweight greased
balloons tossing around our bedroom like fat nasty imps.
Still, it was funny. We poked them, mid-air, at each other.
We laughed and poked them down the stairs and into the
kitchen. We laughed and Harry went to a drawer and picked
out a safety pin, and then he grabbed both balloon-safes
from the air and handed one, mock-solemn now, to me.

"To the freedom of the sperm," he said, and pricked a
hole in the safe I held. "Long live all our babies," and pricked
a hole in his.

"We should give them," he said, "a suitable burial," and
dropped the limp deflated things into the trash.

And now indeed the sperm were free to float around
my body, searching its crannies for the missing part, my
contribution to all this. In bed there was an extra straining,
a willing for the meeting of the parts. Our minds were not
wholly on each other.

As if our child, already existing, was present and waiting
for us to be done, to see if he could step out from behind
the curtains and announce himself.

But always the result was blood.

We were disappointed every month. "Well?" Harry would
ask. We marked the dates on the kitchen calendar, but cryp-

tically, so no one else would know, should anyone, wandering through the kitchen, have noticed. "I'm sorry," I always had to say.

Harry, the impatient one, would only wait six months. "Something should have happened by now," he said. "I'm going to the doctor."

He was so brave, I thought, willing to confront some failure of his body.

Or maybe he could not really imagine that the failure might be his body.

I was not brave when it was my turn. "The doctor says my sperm count's fine. You don't have to go, Edna, it's up to you. But maybe something can be done."

But nothing. "I'm sorry, Mrs. Cormick," the doctor said. "I'm sorry, Harry," I said.

Not fair, to have the blood but not the babies.

"It's all right, Edna," Harry said, but he couldn't help that flash of mourning when I told him. "It's okay. It's not your fault, for God's sake. We can always adopt if we want to. Let's wait and see.

"It's not a tragedy, really. We still have us."

There are no small white darts of stretch marks on my firm body. I look at it, and it's all one piece; has never split, like a cell or an amoeba, into more than itself. And I wonder what is flawed beneath the smooth flesh, where is the piece that is cramped, distorted, and unlinked?

"At least we know," he said.

At least in bed there were just the two of us again, no one else waiting to appear. Something was lost, the extra effort, but something gained as well, knowing there was just us. It was even more important than before to pay attention.

Maybe if I'd had a child and then it had not lived, I could have wept. It's different, not having something you've never had. I just felt — chilly — for a little while. A bit disconnected. When I met women on the street pushing their babies in carriages and strollers I looked and said,

"How sweet," but I didn't really want to touch or hold them. With my own, it would have been different. But my own were locked away.

I see them playing and bouncing around together somewhere inside me, or venturing to whatever the obstacle is and peering beyond and wondering how it would be on the other side. A little longing among them. But like Harry now, they are not whole. They are missing parts of themselves.

Mainly I thought of Harry and his disappointment. His disappointment would be not only for not having a child, but with me as well. For all my efforts, all my work and watching, all my listening hours — I could not be perfect.

We rarely mentioned it, and never again spoke about adoption. I think Harry wanted his own reproduction, not someone else's.

Once he said, "Well, it probably turned out for the best. It would have been quite different with children." (He saw children; I a child.) "We wouldn't have been able to have what we have." By this I do not think he meant a colour television or an expensive stereo or a brand-new car. I think he meant he would not have had my full attention. He got used to that, and mainly liked it. He would not have liked, I think, to have had to share my attention very often.

He might not have liked me holding and rocking a baby for very long.

It hardly matters now.

And of course it's easy to think that things turn out, really, for the best. One cannot imagine how things that never happened might have turned out.

No, that's not true. In some instances, it's beyond belief that some things have been for the best.

I understood that my failures to touch, the fact that I still had no idea of the secret, had even forgotten for some time that there was a secret, meant internal failures as well. Who knew what parts of me might be floating around inside, missing their connections?

These are curious gaps. Now I have nothing to lose. Now I can dare anything, if I want, and merely observe the results. I am no longer susceptible to results.

At lunch there is a woman sitting across the table from me like a mirror image. Her skin is also pale, and I want to know, is there the same feel to it, the same kind of putty sense, as there is to mine? We have been eating in our own solitudes.

I can dare anything right now. My hand goes out to her face, because I am curious about it. I stroke her cheek. It is hot and smooth. She jerks, pulls back. She is more than startled; frightened and fierce as well. When she pulls back it is more than her face, it is her whole body, she stands and her chair tips back behind her onto the floor. She leans forward and swings her arm across the table and crashes her palm across my face. People are running towards us.

It doesn't hurt. It stings a little, but it doesn't seem to have much to do with me. I have felt her skin, and it is warmer than mine; not the same, not the way it looked.

I reached out and I touched her. What might I do next, if it doesn't matter?

I may become a wild woman.

If I did what I felt like doing, what would I do?

They're all strangers here. Where are the people I know, Stella and my parents? The people who might remind me I am not a wild woman. It's too easy, among strangers, to be anybody. I could make me up.

No, I seem to have already done that. Among strangers, I might be the opposite: what I want.

But is that wild, or something else?

I am here an infant of almost forty-four, and may turn into anything. That is not comforting, but a blank.

If I had babies, could they come to see me here? Could I be somebody for them?

I would like to be somebody for someone. It's hard, alone, to be anybody at all. Or easy to be too much, capable of anything.

If I have done what I have done, I am capable of anything.

If I had babies, what would they think of me now? They are so entirely mute inside me; so thoroughly muffled that I could not hear them if they did call out.

What could they tell me? That they forgive me? That they love me anyway?

Now, now I could mourn my missing babies. I would like to feel small arms around me and hear little voices murmuring. I can feel now the tears that were stored away for them; but I still can't weep for Harry.

17

IF I COULD TRACK BACK THROUGH MY DAYS, could I find the spot I missed? It must be somewhere in that house. Under a bed, or in the corner of a closet?

My days were a service, a mass: precise steps and motions, all in order, to the end of either worship or comfort, whichever. Or both.

He never asked me to do it. We never set it out in words. But he must have assumed I was the sort of person who would do all these things, care for him as perfectly as I could, give him all the comfort I was able to. If he hadn't understood that, I think he would not have married me. He wanted, I think, a demonstration of tears and a demonstration of devotion. Although he never said.

A man does not want to waken in the morning to some shrill alarm. I've read it can alter brain waves too abruptly, and in any case it is an unpleasant beginning to the day. Nor does he want to see a haggard, dazed, and tired woman first thing in the morning. Maybe a lot of people can't be bothered worrying about these things. They put themselves first. But not alert Edna, on her toes at all times, double vision seeing always two instead of one.

For years and years my body was trained to wake before the alarm went off, so that I could push the button and prevent the buzzer that would otherwise startle him from sleep. I edged carefully from the bed, so he wouldn't be disturbed. I washed my face and hands, combed my hair, put on my make-up, all in the bathroom.

When I went to wake him, touching him lightly on the shoulder, bending to kiss him, just a little pressure on the forehead was enough, his eyes opened and his first view of the day was me, smiling, cheerful, and ready for the day.

(I wonder how she woke him on those rare nights? They must have been rare; at some point he usually came home, even if after midnight. Was she brisk and careless? Did they get up together, when her face was still printed with the wrinkles of the sheets, her hair strewn about, dishevelled? Did they use the bathroom together, speaking over toilet sounds? I can't bear sharing a bathroom. Even in marriage, especially in marriage, one shouldn't be seen in such private awkward functions.

(Did she make him a proper breakfast, or just throw something together? They must have always been in a hurry, with both of them getting ready for work.

(Would her carelessness have appealed to him? Would he like to be ignored occasionally in the morning? Would he be distressed to find crumbs in the bed, the coffee poorly brewed? I doubt she'd be able to pay much attention, rushing to leave herself.)

The pure intimacy of mornings, alone with the freshness and pursuit of a new day, the prospects of clean clothes and fresh skin and the smells of breakfast, those were things that got me eagerly out of bed.

(What was her apartment like? Elegant? Shabby? Simply thrown together? Did he know which drawer the spoons were in, and where she kept her towels?)

While I made coffee, the smell filling the kitchen, drifting up the stairs — he said he loved that smell — and prepared the breakfast and brought in the morning paper, he was upstairs showering, shaving, I could hear the running water, buzz of razor, sometimes he even sang. Loudly, so that I could hear, even from a distance he could make me laugh, silly songs, "Row, Row, Row Your Boat" from the shower. Banging of drawers, quick steps around the bedroom, I could follow his progress from below, see his stripped slim body adding the layers of clothes, sitting on the bed to pull on socks.

When I heard the clipped steps that meant his shoes were on, I slid the eggs and grease-drained bacon onto his plate, and buttered the toast. There was orange juice already on the table. I poured coffee for myself when he sat down. He shook out his serviette, ate his breakfast, and glanced through the paper. He read some of the stories out to me, the funny or dangerous ones, or the simply amazing. "How can people be like that?" we said, over some story of a parent charged with beating a child. Or "Christ, the transit drivers are going out on strike, the traffic jams will be incredible." Sometimes he read to himself, but if he laughed or grunted and I said, "What? What is it?" he'd read it aloud.

It was a nice beginning to the day. I look back and it was just — nice.

I would see the clock, that white daisy with the yellow centre, yellow hands, moving the minutes to when he would leave. There was so much to be done. He smiled and kissed me and said, "Bye, see you later," and I said, "Have a good day," and stood at the door to wave. I had a small superstition: that if I failed to wave and watch him leave, it would be an unlucky day for both of us.

Methodically, then, my own time got under way. Clearing the breakfast dishes, washing and drying them, wiping the table, the place mats, the counter, the sinks, putting away jams and bread. Sweeping the floor, moving chairs and table out of the way to do so; but that was only surface dirt, small things that might float. To get beneath, a sponge mopping every day, once a month stripped and freshly waxed, so that the kitchen floor was never anything but clean and gleaming.

These things are visible. It was also necessary to search out what might be hidden: make sure there were no crumbs lurking beneath or inside the toaster, and that its silver surface was wiped clear of smudges and distortions. Little bits and pieces of this and that may fall between the counter and the stove: one must not miss the slim alleyways of the house.

Could the hidden spot have been behind the stove, perhaps? Or somewhere behind the fridge? There are so many nooks and crannies where it might be, if I can just put my finger on it.

It only takes a little time for some piece of dirt to tunnel its way to the roots of a carpet. So I vacuumed part of the house each day, so that all of it was done twice a week at least. I know most people do not do that, but don't their carpets rot?

I brushed any dust from table lamps, and then held them up while I polished the wood beneath; used a damp cloth to wipe the glass surface of the coffee table, where there might be Harry's fingerprints, or marks from his heels if he'd put his feet up the night before. Another damp cloth for the white windowsills and the white wood between the panes of glass. And once a week, the panes of glass themselves.

It's amazing how quickly things get dirty even when you try so hard to keep them clean. How filthy they must get when no one pays attention.

The table in the dining room all polished, down on my hands and knees to get at the intricate woodwork underneath, the base and legs. And all around the china hutch. Once a month, all the good dishes came out of the hutch to be washed and dried and put away again, on freshly polished shelves. And again, even in so short a time, dust collected.

It didn't matter that no one else might know or notice that a mysterious and tiny grey wedge of lint and dust might collect in the corner of a shelf in the china cupboard, or that a shred of fuzz — from the sleeve of one of Harry's sweaters? who knew? — might have found its way beneath a couch. I would know. I knew it would distract me. It was easier to deal with it than to have it lurking in my mind.

What on earth was in my mind? All those hours, hands doing their jobs, what was I thinking? Certainly I thought I had plenty on my mind; it must have been the quality that was insufficient. I considered what I'd be doing next, or what I had just done. What food we were running low on, or what I might bake later. How much I would enjoy my bath, and looking forward to a cigarette, a coffee. Some story from the morning paper. A missing child: was it safe? And how were the parents feeling, what were they doing at this very moment, while I went so smugly about my small routines? Would I trade feeling not much for feeling pain? Or what country was bombing which and why, what people were suffering and dying while I was far away and safe? Really safe, in my bomb shelter of a home. Rambling speculations that never came to a conclusion. Curious wanderings, not thoughts. Never sitting down and looking, thoughts only things meandering through the brain while hands did the important jobs.

I also thought about what time it was, how much time was left for this or that, how much time till Harry came home.

I tried not to think of anything before Harry, those days before he came along and picked me up and handed me a life and all these jobs that amounted to a day. If I stopped to think of how it might have been if Harry had not come running up behind me, I shivered. I was grateful to have this work to do.

None of it amounted to thinking. I saved all that for the end.

It always took a long time to vacuum the stairs. That takes so much lifting and shifting of the heavy, awkward machine. But finally upstairs a whole new world, a different set of obstacles to be cleaned away.

More vacuuming, of course, and more polishing of wood. More and larger mirrors too: and there is pleasure in looking at a mirror and seeing undistorted reflection, a pure picture of the room, like a perfect watercolour of a pond.

The bed would be rumpled from Harry throwing back the covers. I stripped off the blankets and the sheets each day, seeing the marks of our bodies vanish. Sheet by sheet and pillowcase by pillowcase, I changed and made up the bed, and we were erased: until the night. In the cold months, the beautiful handmade family quilt was drawn up over it all.

The room that required the most painstaking care, though, was the bathroom. The toilet, for instance, that's something that must be done each day, scrubbed with a disinfectant so that not a single bacteria survives to leap up into our bodies. Who knows, when you can't even see these things, where they might be aiming or what damage they could do?

Wiping also all the outside of the toilet, and then the sink and bathtub; sometimes a Harry hair from one part of his body or another lying in the bottom, a reminder.

Clean towels and washcloths put out; supplies of soap and toilet paper checked daily.

A trip then through the whole house, gathering up items to be washed: Harry's discarded shirt and underwear from the day before, the used towels, washcloths, the night's sheets and my own clothes, a dress or blouse or slacks, and underwear; and downstairs the tea towels used for the dinner, lunch, and breakfast dishes. Everything went to the basement to be sorted, and while the washer was going, I ironed what was washed the day before. A continuous cycle of clean-soiled, soiled-clean. It never ended, but there was a delicious moment each day when I knew everything in the house was clean.

Another trip through the house for garbage. The wicker basket in the bathroom emptied every day and lined freshly with a paper bag. The same thing in the bedroom. And then the heftier amounts from the kitchen, the peelings and tins and coffee grounds: all carried out to the big plastic bags in the garage. Each week Harry would carry those bags out to the street and in the early hours of the next morning they would vanish, and there would be another of those moments when there was nothing dirty in the house.

This was several hours of work, no shirking. And there was a rhythm to it, something stately, like a minuet, a meditation. When it all was done, I allowed myself a cigarette, a coffee, and a salad. My days were dotted with small rewards; and then Harry, the large reward.

What did he do in his office every day that earned him fifteen, twenty, thirty thousand dollars a year? What was it that gave his job such value?

You couldn't gauge my work that way. It wasn't a matter of dollars that could be spent and touched, but of things that might flash by so quickly they could be missed if one weren't watchful: a smile, a touch, a cup of coffee, and a moment to try a quiz in a magazine. A house and a name: Mrs. Harry Cormick.

It wasn't joy I found in housework, but then, there would not be joy in many jobs. Even Harry, in love with his work, felt excitement, not joy. What I felt was — satisfaction, perhaps; duty fulfilled and a debt paid; goodness.

Those magazines with their quizzes and their stories, they underwent small alterations over the years. I began to see small cracks. Once, they spoke of how to keep a husband interested, and gave hints for dealing with household problems. Ways to do things right. More recently they have begun to speak of ways to juggle job and home. They have quick recipes and easy ways of doing housework, instead of thorough ways. I thought, things are being swept aside here. And where would it end? I foresaw chaos, a breaking down.

It seems strange, unfair, that having foreseen that, I should have become the target of chaos and catastrophe. I was so careful. I should have been the last, not the first.

I clipped recipes and glued them onto cards. I went through them, designing dinner, balancing textures and colours and favourites, ingredients and what we had on hand.

It was all organized, and I was comforted to know each step so well. By mid-afternoon a few things would be chopped and simmering, or at least ready to be dealt with. Ingredients would be lined up. I would know where I was going. A couple of times a week, I also baked: cookies, cupcakes, muffins, small things for us to nibble at in the evenings. None of this business of quick dashes of water to dry packaged mixes, either. There's no gift, no sign of caring in that, and I'm sure it must show in the taste.

There was a variety store three blocks away, and if we were low on bread or milk I walked over to get them. The other houses looked more or less like ours. It was a good neighbourhood, quiet and clean. The people were like Harry and me: middle class; professional men and wives, some of whom had jobs. Nothing loud or drastic ever happened, and we were all friendly enough. In the summers, people talked over back fences and shared leftover garden seeds. Sometimes we had barbecues together. In winter, out shovelling, there was a shared comradeship of heavy labour in the cold winds, and one came indoors a bit excited and brisk. When it stormed in the day, I shovelled the drive before Harry came home. Sometimes a neighbour with a snowblower, home early from work, would do it for me. In summer, a woman seeing me heading for the store or going out to pick tomatoes and lettuce for dinner might ask me over for a coffee. We would sit at a picnic table in the back yard and chat. The conversations were not intimate. It was partly, I think, because Harry and I did not have children. The others did. It was a big thing to talk about, and a big thing not to have. It made a space. Also I would not talk about Harry, refused to be drawn into shared confessions, admissions of imperfect lives. Where was the loyalty of those women? Then too, people were transferred, in and out, someone always seemed to be moving. One day to the next, people, like the trash, might vanish.

In late afternoon, the whole house polished and warm with kitchen smells, I went upstairs to get myself ready. Every other day I washed my hair. Every day I had a bath. That was a good time. I took a magazine with me, and my cigarettes, and kept the water piping by turning the hot tap on occasionally with my left foot. I could feel my hard-working muscles unwinding, and my pores opening, cleansing, a drifting possible. But I kept a small clock there, too, on the back of the toilet, in case I drifted too far.

I dried myself, cleaned the tub again, fixed my hair, and dressed. By then it was merely a matter of waiting for the crunching sound of the car in the driveway, the rumble of the garage door opening, the car door slamming, and the garage being closed again, and I was at the door and opening it, a last check of my hair and my make-up in the hallway mirror, and there he was.

Like waving good-bye in the morning: it seemed important to meet him at the door at night. The two acts enclosed my own day.

Really, it's only in the past few years that the routine has altered greatly. Oh, there were some changes along the way. I started adding exercises before my bath in the late afternoon, in my efforts to keep trim. It seems this becomes more difficult with age, however much hard work one may do.

But it's only in the past couple of years that the phone calls have become fairly frequent, Harry saying he'd be late. That the job was taking up his time. That clients from out of town had to be entertained and he'd be staying downtown overnight. His company kept a hotel suite for its executives to be used on such occasions. He was promoted to greater and greater responsibilities, he became an important man in that company. He said the work was therefore trickier and more time-consuming, and required sacrifices of us both. "I don't like wasting my evenings working or taking some dumb asshole out for drinks," he said. "It's just this damned job."

But he was so proud and pleased with himself when he did come home. I would certainly not want to cloud that, I would not complain.

I thought I was wise.

Now I remember him coming home happy from an evening at work, and I recall his pride, and now I know what he was proud of. How could he look at me then and smile and say, "Hi, Edna," and bend to give me a quick hello kiss and say, "Sorry I'm so late. I got tied up"?

It was comforting to have such familiar days. Having found my life, I would not have liked changes or surprises. And if the days were sometimes dull, or if sometimes I would have liked to avoid the work, put it off for some other time, I was proud to overcome that and steel myself and go ahead, plunging through it all. The more I did on such a day, the better, more virtuous I felt. And the closer I felt to Harry, because it was done for him, for us.

At the end of a day I was warm with satisfaction.

I seem to have had a great deal of pride, after all.

It is strange now to see those twenty years. A great long chunk of life in the past, it's like a package. And not, as I might have expected, all ribbons and pretty wrapping; from a distance, stripped of what I thought it meant, brown paper tied with string. And although I know it seemed right at the time, from a distance it weighs a ton. It was made up of such light small things, too — it's a puzzle.

It also seems primitive, superstitious, and innocent. Each task a kind of ritual abasement, an appeasing of unknown, threatening gods, a sacrifice like slaughtering goats on altars to fool the gods. They are offered gifts and are diverted. Or like saying prayers on beads, or making certain movements in particular ways, a form of worship and of fear. Holding up the cross to a vampire?

And somehow I missed a step, a sacrifice, a bead. I missed something.

I would like not to know. I would take all that weight back if I could be given not knowing again. I could go back and find out what I missed and I could take care of it and none of this would happen. I would be content. And I would work much, much harder to make it perfect.

18

I SEE I STILL TRY to hold onto secrets, even when there is no one to keep them from any more except myself, and what's the point of that?

If Harry had secrets, I had one, too. My addiction, my single lapse from duty. A hidden sweet in the afternoon.

I remain guilty and embarrassed about it. Because it was a self-indulgence? Perhaps because it may have been the flaw.

It was that at some point (when, exactly?) I returned, with a mixture of reluctance and unease and pleasure, to that old habit, my comfort going back to childhood, of lying silent and eyes closed, separated by blindness from where I was, listening to the music and stealing it for myself. I sang on the stage again, and danced around the same old polished floors, this time with an elegant Harry, a face to the figure now, while other people watched admiringly.

I stole to the couch in the afternoon and put albums on the record player and turned up the volume. A grown woman doing this, the same as she had in that old university apartment before Harry arrived to take up the evenings with his hard lean words and body.

But my body and voice were so free and loud in someone else's body and voice. I might ask, "Why do I do this?" and say, "I won't do it again, there's something wrong about it," as if it were a kind of masturbation, but would be lured back another day by how it felt. Blood rejoicing, muscles shifting beneath the skin as it went on before my eyes.

Oh, I was important: I sang for my family and danced in front of Harry's friends. Sometimes in a concert, sometimes on a small club stage. Wherever, they looked and admired. I was someone. I was anyone: from Streisand to Baez I could claim anyone's voice I chose, for my own small neat body. Musicals were best, from the *South Pacific* and *Oklahoma* of the early days to *Hair* and *Jacques Brel*, because I could dance in them as well as sing. Sometimes, when musicals were out of fashion, they were difficult to find and I fell back on the old favourites. Sometimes, as in the dancing, Harry became a voice with mine, because after all, with my eyes closed I could do anything, even make him someone else.

He used to say, flipping through the albums, "Jesus, we have a lot of stuff by women here," and it was true. I fed my cravings with occasional new albums, and if there was no musical that appealed, I chose something with a woman's voice that I could transform into mine.

Most often I placed him in the audience, where he sat watching proudly and with amazement, like the others.

Sometimes I found myself smiling. The trick has always been to keep the eyes closed. If they flickered open in the middle of a song, before the time was right, there was a flash of startled pain. It was a shock to see my clean cool living room when I was sweating from the dance inside.

It was never for very long. When an album ended, I resumed my day. The feeling was odd, though, when it was done: both satisfied and a bit dissatisfied, a little shaken and bewildered and uneasy. But by then it didn't matter much because there were only easy things left to do: exercise and take a bath and change my clothes, greet Harry. The music was for when the work was done. And maybe it wasn't so awful a weakness, nothing as bad as drinking or eating a bag of cookies all at once. It wasn't anything that showed. Just an old familiar dream that gave me, for a little time, my old familiar second life. It was enough; I always knew I wouldn't like it to be real, all those people staring, and certainly knew that the life I had was the one I wanted.

Still, it may have been the flaw: that for a half-hour or so in a day I was someone else and had those longings. Maybe it was far too often and for far too long. Maybe, most of all, it was a secret.

I wonder if Harry also had some hidden life inside his head? What did he see when he closed his eyes and listened?

And I wonder if she also had dreams of being someone else, just for a little while. Maybe she even dreamed of being me.

19

THE MAGAZINES SAID, "Rate your marriage — how close are you *really*?" Or, "The women in his office — what you have that they don't."

They had quizzes, which were irresistible: "When your husband comes home from work, do you a) greet him at the door with a smile; b) call hello to him but leave the vacuum cleaner running; c) greet him at the door by telling him what a terrible day you've had?"

I scored well on all the quizzes. "How to be more attractive for your man," I read. "How to be sure he'll always come home."

"Men fear age," they said. "They fear a loss of power, question waste and futility, and may go through phases. Be patient," they said.

But I was frightened, too. I didn't want to be old either. What phases did I have? How would his aging be different or worse than mine?

They didn't say.

When I was not quite thirty, I looked in the bathroom mirror one day and saw suddenly, as if they'd appeared overnight or had had a special light thrown on them, that my hair now included a few distinct grey slivers. My shining hair already dying.

I leaned over the spotless sink, staring; chose one and plucked it from the surrounding brown. It came out painlessly: a sign of dead hair, death, to be able to pull it without pain. It was a perfect total gleaming silver. I was surely not so old? So much of my time couldn't be gone? My days were all the same, what had happened, what event, that could make some hair turn silver? Nothing that I could see. I should be perfectly preserved and young.

That curling silver hair clung to my fingers like a prophecy. It didn't seem right to drop it in the trash as if it could be dismissed. Dangerous, even, to fail to see. Ten years with Harry gone. What did that mean, that there was so little to remember?

I looked at my face and it seemed to have melted somehow; features indistinct, a sort of pudding.

I would have to fix that; start exercising, the pat-patting beneath the chin and all the rest.

When I did turn thirty, Harry, two years older, said, "Don't worry, it's a snap." For him, it had been. He was still gaining power, not yet near the stage when he might fear losing it.

For me, that birthday came at a time when people ten years younger were saying things like, "Don't trust anybody over thirty." A dividing line established, a dividing line between me and young. And between me and these strange people coming up behind with their cold and revolutionary eyes.

"Of course," said Harry, "these kids have a lot to learn. They'll see."

Was it not what he'd expected when he was twenty, then?

(That woman, that girl, she would have been only what, thirteen or so, when I turned thirty. A baby, a child. An entirely different world, hers, I suppose.)

No one came to my home with lights and television cameras to see how I lived. No writers came with pads and pens to ask me my principles, what my solutions were.

No, they all talked to those younger ones, who were so sure. Even at their age I had not been sure, and I watched them on television and read their words in magazines with amazement. They marched, those girls, young women, in demonstrations, and some were even wanted by the police. They were terrifying. Some of them were also beautiful.

Their words, the things they did — they were saying I did not exist. They threatened my life with their demands.

And my magazines were altering, and there were new ones besides, entirely foreign. My mother, now, she might have liked them.

Unsettling enough turning thirty, without the rules changing also.

It was odd not to be young. Not old, of course, but also no longer young. I woke up in the mornings sometimes assuming an enormous future, and realized it was not so enormous any more. My body still seemed young, grey hairs or no. It was trim and firm. But there I was, thirty, a contradiction. I must have assumed that body and mind and time and everything would move together, synchronized. It was a shock to find one leaping ahead of the others.

I found myself thinking, "So this is it."

But where did that thought come from? I had what I wanted. It was not as if I'd had dreams of anything so very different, or ambitions to be something else. I had never considered seriously other possibilities. But it was still unsettling, disquieting, to think that now there would not be any.

Why did I think thirty was so old? Now it seems quite young.

I can still be surprised when I wake up some mornings wondering who I'll be. Now, of course, it's a fair question: who will I be?

I can't apologize, although it seems one is expected to these days, for spending twenty years caring for my husband and my home. Could I explain that was just my way of caring for myself?

My cause was not as spectacular as the ones of those people on television parading for civil rights and against war, for equal rights and against killing seals. My cause did not make for parades in the streets.

But if a civil-rights marcher is assaulted by a black, if an animal-lover is bitten by a dog, or an equal-rights demonstrator attacked by a woman, what does that mean? That all those efforts, those fair feelings, have gone to waste? In the victim, is there a sense of betrayal, a resentment that one's energy was stolen, one's caring disregarded?

Whose fault is it? Some ultimate uncaring selfishness in the attacker, a blindness? Or a flaw in the giver, who gives not quite enough. Who fails to give quite everything. Whose fault are these breakdowns, anyway?

"Look," I said to Harry, "if you want to work this weekend, go ahead. I'll find things to do." He'd spread out his papers on the glass-topped coffee table in the living room. I took him tea and sandwiches and opened his beer for him. He had to concentrate, so I read quietly in the kitchen, or did some baking. I wanted to let him be, when that was what he wanted.

But I never meant him to assume I wasn't there. I didn't mean to disappear.

My magazines, the ones I liked and was raised on, made it seem so clear. If one did this, that would result. Did I not follow the instructions carefully enough? I never could put things together. Harry bought kits for building things: a worktable or a set of shelves, and he could fit piece A into slot B with no difficulty at all, perceiving the logic of the thing. Me, I would have been left with a pile of unconnected pieces.

I thought — what did I think? That I had a home and Harry and so I was safe. I would be terrified without them.

I am terrified.

I didn't lie. If I turned my efforts into making him important, that was true. What I demonstrated to him of devotion was a mere glimmer of the truth.

When did the lie begin? His lie. Certainly not from the beginning. Perhaps only quite lately, which means that for most of those years there was no lie, those years are genuine. Maybe he just got tired. Or bored. I knew how easily bored he was in other ways.

Oh, I want him here. I have so many questions and he's the only one who knows. Why? I would say. What did I do wrong? What were you looking for? What more could I have done? When did it start?

Lunch is scalloped potatoes, thawed peas, a slice of ham, a dish of custard. Coffee, too, or tea. The potatoes are a little soggy, the peas wrinkled, the ham somewhat over-cooked, the custard bland, the coffee bitter. It's not an awful meal, just not a good one.

What I miss about it is not taste. What is lacking is a complete meal on my table. What I would like to see is a whole dish of potatoes from which to scoop my own, an entire ham or turkey or roast sitting there waiting to be carved.

What we are served are individual plates of food, each as if it has come from nowhere, has no origins. A little inhuman, to have it presented this way. Food should be part of a whole, a ceremony of care.

I wonder what's happened to all my recipes? All those clippings from magazines, pasted or copied so carefully onto file cards. And the recipe books that I used to read, thumbing through the pages and pictures, selecting, balancing, visualizing the combinations of possibilities on our plates.

I wonder what's happened to all my things? The house? Can it just be sold, without my ever seeing it again? Because I don't want to go back. I do not ever want to be inside that yellow kitchen with the white and yellow daisy clock. I do not want to see that living room with its wall of white gold-flecked paper, and I do not want to be upstairs. The pillows alone would break my heart.

Is someone looking after it? If not, will the pipes freeze this winter, or the furnace break down? By now dust must be gathered on the windowsills, and there will be bits of fluff and dirt settled in the carpets.

It seems it should be wrong, after a twenty-year investment of effort and work and attention, not to care. But I do not care. Let the place fall down.

I can think of only one thing about it that might give me

pleasure now. I think that if I were out of here I might drive a bulldozer to that house and smash it into splinters. That, I think, might give me joy.

I see that for all this tidy writing, following so carefully the lines, the rage is still there, in the ink and in the movements of the tendons of my hands.

20

"TALK TO ME, EDNA," he'd say. "What did you do today?"

Well, I felt contented, and pleased with myself. But to tell him what I had done — I could do these things an infinite number of times, it seemed, but I could hardly describe them an infinite number of times.

The trick with housework is to make one's labours invisible, so that the other person does not observe them, but would observe their absence.

We talked about vacation plans, food we liked, a new restaurant to try or a movie to see, articles in newspapers, and programs on TV. He said, "Okay to have the Baxters over Saturday? Could you maybe make those little quiches?"

"What about your day?" I asked. "How did it go?"

He was in the marketing department of a drug firm. He ended up head of it. Was he pleased with that? Might he have concluded he wasted his gifts on so small a stage?

A stage, yes. I can see him as an actor, someone striding and declaiming, or hunched and whispering to the farthest rows. Laughing, head thrown back, or weeping, face in hands.

This is no criticism, that he was alert to the effects of alterations in tone of voice or sudden movements. It was a skill he had, a gift, an offshoot of the intensity with which he saw his life, himself, and of his wish to be in charge. If someone had said, "What a liar he is," instead of "What a performer," I would not have understood.

I'm sure that for him it felt quite different to act than to lie. One for his pleasure, the other for his preservation.

But the skill in lies must have been cultivated in the acting.

What if he had truly been an actor? Would that have satisfied his desire to play out roles? Would he have known the difference between the play and all the rest?

I see him furious; dismissive; amused; bored. He could be all those things in our living room, with our company. I could watch the people watching him and listen to the changes in their words and voices. He changed topics with just a sigh and a shifting of his weight.

I thought I could appreciate his performances and still see the husband Harry underneath.

I thought he spoke to me in different ways. For one thing, I never heard tenderness except with me. He could be gentle and kind with others, but not tender. To me he might say, "Edna, you're perfect," although that might be in connection with a special meal for guests or in a quiet moment in our bedroom.

We could spend evenings doing very little except reading or watching television. He stretched out on the couch. He didn't need to speak unless he wanted to. It was a sign of trust, that he could relax so far with me. He trusted me, and therefore no performance.

With all the others he had to be on his toes.

But I, too, could be an actress. A silent, listening actress.

How many hours in twenty years did I spend listening? Nodding, asking questions (but that was part of listening). He spoke with such enthusiasm of his work and confided his manipulations. Another sign of his trust, that he could still talk freely of moves made with selfish, sometimes cruel, motives. I might listen with some pity for a man squeezed out, or injured in some Harry-feint. The effects didn't seem real to him. His pleasure was in the game itself, it seemed, no meaning for him beyond that.

What he told me was not real to me, either. More like stories read in magazines or heard on radio. Not even as real as a television program.

"You know what you need in business, Edna?" he asked. "You need the right image. Of course you can't make too many mistakes, either, but a lot of it is how people see you. You can get away with more mistakes for a longer time if they think you're a winner, but if you're not confident about yourself or let them think you're not dead sure of what you're doing, it doesn't matter how many things you do right — they think you're a loser. It's a hell of a lot better to risk the odd mistake and make quick decisions and be definite about it than to hesitate. I'm good, you know. I'm really good at that."

"I know."

"You also have to make them notice you. You have to have a character in their minds. Not weird, of course, or eccentric, I don't mean that. But you have to stand out."

All that was somewhere else. In our two-person corporation, we didn't have to worry about these things.

I had, however, a few betraying thoughts. (Were they the missed spots? Certainly a sign of imperfection.) Sometimes when he was very keyed up from a particular move and went over and over it aloud at home, crowing and analysing, I was bored. And amazed at being bored, so unlikely for me, who could spend days and years in the same routines. And I might think, "He sounds so *young*." I meant, I think, that he wanted so much praise.

(Did she praise him? She was so much closer to that part of him; did she say, "Great work, Mr. Cormick, you handled that so well"? When would the Mr. Cormick have changed to Harry? Did they talk business over wine and dinner? She, who was right there, must have had a special view. Maybe when she praised him, it meant more from her than from me, because she would really know.)

I understood, with some surprise, that I protected him and gave him balance. "He needs me here, too," I thought.

I fed him that way and others. He fed me with his long arm around my shoulder when I woke up, my head in the dent where his shoulder met his chest when I fell asleep.

And too, there was his energy, the heat that flowed out of him and into me. I didn't think I raised much heat on my own.

Sometimes, yes, I might have liked to say, "Let's talk about something else for a while." But what? He said, "Talk to me, Edna," but what about?

I might have liked to say, "Harry, I don't understand. I know you're good, but I'm not there, I don't see it. It wearies me to hear all this."

That would have broken something. Everything, I suspect.

Did he only love my ears then? Surely there was more.

His beautiful smile, white teeth between narrow lips, the kind of lips to look at and remember how they feel; the creases of laughter by his mouth, the crinkles around his eyes.

We laughed, too. We enjoyed ourselves. In any magazine, this was a good marriage.

When I put on four or five pounds and told him I was going to start exercising and eating a little less, he looked at me, mock-solemn, like a doctor. "Stand up," he said, "and turn around." Then, "Come here, let me examine," and he poked my ribs, my stomach, my thighs, my arms, said, "Fat are you? Where? Here? Is this where you're fat? Or here?" and he pulled me down onto him, both of us laughing, on the couch.

Sometimes he was angry. But with Harry, anger wasn't very serious. He did not like to keep things bottled up inside. He let them out and then forgot.

He said, on a hot day in summer, "For Christ's sake, are we out of lemonade? You might know we'd need a lot in this weather. What the hell do you do all day, anyway?"

That sort of thing. Not often. But when he got tired. Sometimes just office irritations slipping into home. I could understand that.

"Jesus Christ, that goddam Baxter. Can't piss without getting his zipper stuck. What an asshole. Why is my life full of assholes?"

Because, I think, he liked it that way. Because he wanted to be the best. Because I stroked his hair, the back of his neck, and listened to him, and made his drinks.

But surely I wasn't lying, not really. Acting, on occasion, perhaps, but not lying.

God, to have ever said what was true.

This business of anger, it frightened me. Not Harry's sort: that hurt me, but did not frighten.

And I was right. I was right to feel my own rage might lead anywhere.

How often did my father swallow fury as he opened the door to the porch to have his pipe out there in the cold and the wind? Or, for that matter, how many times did my tense and, I think now, ambitious mother bite her tongue against complaints and urgings that he be better, bigger somehow. Because she didn't press him that way; merely bullied him in small ways.

Maybe in that house suppressed rage was seeping out of them like leaking gas and was inhaled by the wood, the wallpaper, and the linoleum. Maybe I breathed it in, along with fear. Maybe we were all poisoned by the air.

If ever, in my parents' house, someone had truly spoken and the anger had emerged from the woodwork and the linoleum, surely the walls would have crumbled, the roof collapsed, the glass windows shattered.

To have ever said the truth to Harry.

What was the truth, to be so terrifying?

That sometimes I looked at him across the living room at night, or watched him sleeping in our bed, and wondered, "Who is this man?"

Did he glance at me sometimes too and mistake me for a stranger? Did he find my burden boring?

But where did the final fury come from?

I wish to record the colour of carrots on the plate, the softness of potatoes, the quality of meat. For the second course, the doughiness of pie crusts, the dryness of cakes, the seeds in the fruits. I would catch in words the doctor's voice, the coolness of water warming in the throat, the tightness of a comb tugging through hair, pulling at the roots.

I lived with a man for twenty-odd years. Here, the only man I see is the doctor, twice a week.

He is quite different from Harry, it seems, although sometimes I feel an inclination to rest against him, to trust him in a similar way. But I no longer have faith in my own assessments.

I have no firm reason to believe he wouldn't lie to me.

He is still young — a decade younger than Harry. He has fine blond hair, cut moderately long so that it often catches on his shirt collar and I would like to brush it free. He has a habit, when he's talking, asking all those questions, of flicking his head so that the hair tosses back from his forehead.

The backs of his hands have fine hair on the knuckles, just as Harry's did. Are there similar hairs, equally soft-looking, on his chest, his legs, perhaps even his back? He dresses so carefully. He wears suits and shirts and ties, and although the ties are sometimes loosened at the throat, the shirts are always buttoned to the top, allowing no glimpse of flesh. And his socks are pulled high so that even when he sits in that listening pose, leaning forward, right ankle resting on left knee, with the tautness of trousers following the angles of his legs, no calf or ankle shows. Except for his face and hands, he keeps his skin to himself.

The hair on his head and knuckles seems so fine and soft it isn't possible to imagine a proper beard. His face would only grow more silky hair.

There is nothing harsh about him; even his voice is gentle.

What about anger then? Does he shout at home? I can't imagine; but then, who can tell?

He has slender hands and long fingers, but although they remind me of Harry's, I could not mistake them. There are blue veins prominent beneath the skin, and his finger-nails are clean and neatly clipped. He is so clean he has no scent of even aftershave or soap.

His eyes are immensely blue and deep. They invite me to dive in. They look as if they're waiting. It feels almost safe, looking into them, because I don't see anything back.

I'm pleased when he stops in to my room, or when a nurse says, "Come on now, Mrs. Cormick, time to see the doctor." I stand quickly, eagerly, then dawdle to hide my anticipation.

Sometimes he has new clothes and I like that: he has pride in his appearance. His shirts are always crisply ironed, so either his wife takes care of him well or he takes them to a laundry. Many people do, these days. So many things are easier, or ignored, these days.

His arms are long and his body is thin. Like Harry's, his wrists show bones. Also like Harry, he stands straight. (Although in the last few years, Harry was starting to stoop a little, as if his shoulders were becoming heavy. Perhaps this doctor will come to that.)

Sometimes I see him in the hall, going past my door, and if he sees me notice, he smiles. But he does not stop unless he has planned a visit. He does not walk quickly, but seems always to be on his way somewhere. I would like to know where all he goes.

What I would like sometimes would be to put my arms around him and set my head against the solid bones of his chest. I would like to touch the softness of his hair.

Instead I sit in a chair across his desk from him, and write these wishes down.

It's snowing. For the first time this year. The flakes melt and disappear as soon as they land against the window and the earth. What happens? Do they turn into something else, or simply vanish? I should be able to see it happen, the transformation of one thing into something else. It looks solid, the snow, coming down, and suddenly it's gone and just the greyness of the day is left. If it fell on me, surely I could touch it so gently there'd be no need for it to vanish. I might at least get close enough to see.

21

STELLA, NOW, IMAGES OF MY SISTER dance by now and then as I sit here. Which is funny, since I rarely thought of her once I got away. Once I didn't have to watch her easiness, like someone eating a bowl of strawberries and refusing to share, I mostly forgot.

Of course I only knew her as a child. Those are my memories.

I thought events would not touch my sister, who would always dance over disaster. Or stare it in the teeth the way she did my mother, and defy it. Even as a little girl, I remember her stamping her foot, her tiny fists planted on her hips, a miniature of my mother's stance, and saying, "No. I don't want to. I won't."

She got spanked. I slid along being quiet and obedient and observing.

We seemed to have nothing in common.

In high school she was one of those swift-footed golden people who knew the steps.

But then — then it seemed to me that after I left home, because I worked at school and I was bright enough, or needy enough, to be sent away, the tables turned. The advantage on my wedding day was mine.

And she, my bright-haired laughing sister, married a young plumber and they bought a little house just three blocks from my parents, and when Harry and I visited at Christmas I was the one with what they may have thought was a life with some glamour.

I was not a different person from the one they knew; but it was a great deal, enough, to seem to be a different person.

It may have astonished them to see me with this driving man who talked with passion about things they didn't even think about. A businessman talking to a plumber and a retired hardware clerk.

Of course it isn't that we were better, nothing so mean or pretentious. Just that against every expectation I married a man with a career and a future and moved on to the city and an unfamiliar life, while there was Stella, at home with her plumber. If things had been as they appeared, surely it would have been the reverse? Stella, the sparkling hostess, with the dazzling husband; me, the small-space person, with the plumber in the town. If with anyone at all.

"Lovely to see you," we said at Christmas and brushed cheeks lightly with our lips.

"Honest to God," Harry said as we drove home afterward, "it's like being with a bunch of strangers trapped in a storm. Nobody says anything. Don't you have anything to say to each other?"

No, we didn't. Scratch the surface and a maelstrom underneath? None of us had the will for that, certainly not I.

We talked, Stella and my mother and I, about clothes, new stores in town, and recipes. Small problems with our homes, redecorating. I doubt these domestic details were particularly satisfying, to my mother especially, but there we were, three adult women thrown together for a day or two, what would we talk about? The question for my mother would have been, "What made you so stiff and unhappy and stern?" For my sister it might have been, "What is that secret you knew? Why did it always go so smoothly?" And maybe they would have had questions for me as well.

No chance we would say things like that.

"That old saying about shoemakers' children going barefoot is just about true at our place," Stella complained. "We've had a dripping kitchen tap for weeks, and Frank never gets around to doing a thing about it. I'm going to have to call a plumber, if you can believe it."

My mother never tried to set rules for Harry or Stella's Frank, she must have had some respect for them, so when they sat down with my father in the living room and pulled out cigarettes, my father found courage to light up his pipe. His annual treat, this holiday defiance. He never looked entirely comfortable about it, his pleasure was uneasy, but he did it.

After they went to bed, my mother sprayed the room and washed the blue-glass candy dishes they used as ashtrays.

"Why do we do this every year?" Harry asked.

I don't know. We spent Thanksgiving with his parents, and sometimes Easter. But Christmas with mine. Nothing to do with fairness or equal time, I think. But Christmas would have been strange to me anywhere else. Unhappy sometimes, and always odd, but it smelled right, the only time in the year that house smelled friendly instead of damp. The onions and spices and turkey, cranberry bubbles and gravy and mincemeat pies — nowhere else would have had the right smells.

Christmas sent me back to childhood, made me childish. I remember for years there were dolls, one for me and one for Stella, unwrapped, under the tree from Santa Claus. Christmas Eve the four of us would sit in the darkened living room, only the coloured tree lights on, and stare at them. Mute, of course. Stuck in our own thoughts. But there we were, the four of us. Maybe we were all waiting for somebody to say something. Maybe every Christmas for years afterward we went back there to sit and wait for somebody to say something. In any case, whoever else was added, Harry, Frank, we'd started off, the four of us, together, and there was a sort of inescapable life sentence about it.

But where are they now? Have I gone too far and been abandoned?

It could be they just don't know what to say.

We wrote letters to each other occasionally, in a sort of three-way futility. My mother about neighbours, the weather, a new lampshade, her small attempts to do something with the house. "Your father's well," she always ended. "He sends his best." She signed herself, "Mother." I wrote about Harry and his work and the changes in our house, the company we had for dinner or the party we might be going to.

Stella covered much the same ground as my mother, as well as bits of news about people we both knew from our school days. "Mother and Dad are well," she said. "Bored with each other and miserable as usual."

We might have talked about them, maybe, Stella and I. Certainly they were what we had in common. We were never alone together though. First our parents, then our husbands. I have never sat across a kitchen table just talking with my sister over a cup of coffee. I have never sat out on a porch and smoked a cigarette just with her. We have only written letters and stared into space.

But she tried. Once, she tried, and for a little while afterward. It's that effort that makes me think that if she walked into this room right now, I might put down the pen and the notebook and let her put her arms around me, if she would.

Now, I would certainly have things to say. And now no reason not to.

I guess when she wrote me that letter, it would have been a little like that for her. And I failed her. Would she fail me? For revenge, if nothing else? I see now what she may have meant, but I didn't then, I couldn't imagine. And I am sorry, Stella. That's the first thing I would say to her now: I'm sorry, I didn't know.

Then I would say, but I do now, and we might compare notes and tell each other how it felt. Of course it worked out better for her, quite differently. Because she knew how to stamp her feet and put her fists on her hips and say no? Because she had long practice at defiance and survival? Well, if she came to see me here, we could maybe discuss that sort of thing.

A fat, scrawled letter it was, the handwriting not quite recognizable as hers. I finished my morning's work and sat down with my coffee and cigarette to read it. There was never any urgency about the mail.

She always wrote on notepaper just like her: little pink and mauve and white flower bunches on the top left-hand corner of each sheet, a matching mauve envelope. One would expect a lilac scent to float from it. Usually there were two neatly filled sheets; this time a bundle, different.

"Dear Edna," up by the flowers. Green ink. She always used green ink.

"Dear Edna, This will come as a surprise, but to come right to the point, I'm leaving Frank. I've been putting off writing you about it because it's hard to put down like that, it's like saying somebody's dead, but I've known long enough now, I'm used to the idea in a funny sort of way, so now I can write it down. This is the first time, I'm practising on you, because one of the hard things about it is actually telling people. They don't sell cards so you can just announce it. Not that I'm telling people everything, just that I'm leaving and what my plans are, but you'd be surprised (maybe you wouldn't) how nosey and rude people can be. It's all over town, of course you know people here don't have anything much better to do than talk. Mother is totally humiliated, so she's furious with me. Not with Frank, even though it's his fault, but with me because I've made a thing about it so everybody knows. She wouldn't even tell you.

"Anyway, to get to what happened, do you remember my best friend in high school, Carol? She and her husband Tony and Frank and I have chummed around for years. A couple of weeks ago Tony called me and said did I know Carol and Frank were having an affair. Of course I didn't, so you can imagine how shocked I was. But he had all the proof, dates and times and even a note from Frank to Carol setting something up, he's so stupid, although I guess I should be glad he is because otherwise I mightn't have ever found out. Tony kicked the crap out of Carol and I just packed Frank's things and told him to get lost. It's bad enough he was screwing around, but with my best friend!

When I think about it, I'm more upset with her than I am with him, I mean friends shouldn't do that, should they? I don't see how a friend could. And I mean, what is Frank anyway, just some dumb plumber, why should she want him so much, he's not so hot. Well, she's got him now, for good if she wants him.

"Mother says, you surely didn't have to make him leave. You can live with a lot of things. Well, maybe she can, but I don't intend to spend the rest of my life with any guy who can do a thing like that. Once something like that starts it doesn't stop, and besides, my best friend! I can't get over that. I don't ever want to lay eyes on him again, and as for living with him!

"Pretty soon, this is the rest of my plan, I won't have to lay eyes on him ever again, because I'm leaving town. We have to do a bunch of legal stuff, of course, and I'm making him pay through the nose for this, believe me, but as soon as all the papers are signed, I'm taking off. It's funny, but now I'm almost used to what's happened and having everything all of a sudden go all ass over teakettle, I'm kind of excited. Like for the first while I just hurt, that's all I could think about, and then I was furious, but then I started to think, well, to hell with it then, and after a while I got to wondering about what I'd do next. There's only a certain amount of time you can spend not doing anything, after all.

"So I thought and thought, and it dawned on me I'm free. I'm not so old, and I can start again. I'll have enough money from Frank to give me a breathing space and a chance to get on my feet and I don't feel bad about that because by God he owes me.

"Anyway, what I'm pretty sure I'm going to do is move out to Vancouver. The first thing about being free is not being here, that's for starters, so I looked at a map and I thought, Vancouver. At least it's supposed to be warm. No more of these lousy winters. And it seems it might be far enough away that everything really might be different. Can you imagine, Edna, everything all of a sudden being different? It's like getting a chance to be a new person.

"It's funny, though, the dumb things you miss. I guess they'll go away. But for instance not having to have Frank's supper on the table at six, that makes the whole hour between five and six a little weird, like there's just no *reason* to do certain things any more. It's really strange sleeping alone, that's hard to get used to, because you're so used to having somebody else there, it's like the bed's out of balance. And I don't have to get up at the crack of dawn, so I've been sleeping in sometimes till nine and then I wake up and lie there wondering what the hell I have to do that means I should haul myself out of bed. There are all these things I never thought about before. Like why *did* I used to get up so early? Just because he had to get up. It makes you wonder about all the other things you did, just because of somebody else.

"Now I'm free, though, and whatever I do from now on is going to be for me. The hell with sacrifice.

"I get so damn mad when I think about it. It sets me off, just thinking about getting up to put a good breakfast into him so he'll have lots of energy to get through the day, and then he goes off to screw Carol.

"The other thing is, you lie around wondering what you did wrong and what you should have done so he wouldn't have to go running off to somebody else. But then I think, so what? Maybe he's just a bastard. Why should I kill myself trying to hold onto somebody like that? I mean, he ought to owe me something too, he should have put some effort into this.

"And then Mother tells me things are never quite what you might want in a marriage, and you have to just get used to that and live with it. At least she can't say think of the children because thank God we don't have any and maybe if we did I'd agree with her and decide to stick it out for them. But I don't see any need to suffer just to keep Frank and his pay cheque rolling in. I don't want Frank rolling in at all, and I can always learn to take care of my own money, I expect. With some off the top from him to get me started.

"Poor Mother. It makes me wonder what she put up with. Heaven knows Dad wouldn't have been screwing around, but she's right, there's always something. She sighs a lot. She always sighed a lot, but now she sighs all the time. I bet she gets up in the morning and looks out the window and sighs.

"Lucky, you, you got away. I probably shouldn't say this, it'll likely sound awful, but I was always jealous of you. It wasn't your fault, but I always remember Mother saying stuff like, Why can't you be like Edna and just be good? and Edna works hard in school, you could get good marks too if you worked hard. She was right, too, I could have gotten away to university maybe, and everything would have been different if I'd had better marks, but you don't think about those things when you're just a kid having fun. And now you're all settled down in a nice house with a nice smart husband and you can do whatever the hell you want. So sometimes, I have to tell you, I think, How come Edna got everything right and it turns into such a mess for me? It's my own fault, of course, but now I'm going to go out and get what I want and I'm not going to make a mess of things again.

"Sometimes I wish we could sit down and talk. We seem miles apart. I guess we are. Now I don't have a best friend any more, it's kind of lonely. I guess you don't realize how few people you can really talk to until something like this happens. What it comes down to is, old happy-go-lucky Stella doesn't have a soul she can tell her troubles to. Sounds like a song, doesn't it?

"I'm not going to be able to get all this into the envelope if I don't stop. I'll write again and let you know what's happening and when I'm leaving, and maybe we can work in a visit before I go. I don't know what time there's likely to be and just how much money I'm going to be able to get out of Frank. Anyway, I feel better now for sitting down and writing it to you. It makes it realer to me.

"See you, big sister. Love, Stella."

Well. I read it again slowly, to take it all in. Sorting the facts and the feelings from the odd sense of a plea running underneath it all.

In every possible way, this was an astonishing letter. Because of the news itself, for one thing. Who would have dreamed all this from a dull lumbering man like Frank? In that dull lumbering town.

And with a best friend? I have had no opportunity to test any theory I might have about best friends, but I imagined closeness and trust. I thought Harry must be my best friend, a compact relationship that included everything.

I read the letter again. The fact that it was from Stella, and to me, was also astonishing.

All those Christmases and recipes and bits of gossip and all those evenings watching my golden sister dance out the door — and instead of that, this was Stella? Stella was also proud and lonely and hurt and excited and — most amazing to me — envious? Envious of me?

There had never been anything to indicate that she was even particularly interested, much less envious.

And why should she be? My dreams were of Stellahood. Given them I would be a blonde with flying feet and laughing eyes and easy conversation. I might still have Harry, but I would be someone else.

But I was not that sort of person. And she was right, things did work out for me, I had what I had wanted. The rest was only a dream.

She felt a little guilty about what happened? A little that it might be her fault, Frank going off like that? Well, it sounded reasonable. She must have missed something, true enough, he would surely not do it for no reason at all. There must have been something lacking in her. I admit to a little nudge of pleasure, seeing she could not be perfect. Not nice, but there it is.

But then she could skip past that, could divert herself from searching for the flaw. She could dismiss whatever her fault might have been and not try to make it up or correct it. She could say, "But now I'm free."

Free? But how was she bound? How terrible can it be, how great an infringement, to get up early to make a breakfast, or to concentrate on dinner? Like Harry, she called me free. I suppose they were right, in a way. But I didn't know what it meant. Stella did, she learned. She was excited by it. If I thought of freedom, I saw chaos; a great black catastrophic pit in which anything could happen.

And Stella was excited by it?

She could look at a map and point at a city and suddenly, bang, she would go there and live. A new start, a different life. She thought that would amaze me, that possibility? It horrified me. What if such a thing could happen? "What if Harry died?" I thought, for it was all I could imagine.

Oh, the things I would have asked her, right then. And more things I would ask her now.

I read the letter again and again, trying to understand. When Harry came home I showed it to him. Relieved, because knowing so much, he would know this as well, would be able to analyse it for me at a glance.

"Too bad," he said. "Dirty trick. Sounds as if Stella's right though, getting out while she still can. She's young enough to start again. Surprising though. I didn't know the bastard had it in him."

Was there a touch of admiration there? I didn't hear it.

"Doesn't it seem funny to you that she can just leave? And she feels free? Doesn't that sound wrong somehow?"

"Well, it isn't all she feels, after all. And no, I can't see it's wrong to feel free. No, not really." I hear those words now, his tone — I listen.

"But," and this was what I really wanted him to explain, "to think of her envying me!"

"Well," and he smiled, "you're a pretty enviable person. You've got me, and that alone . . ." We laughed, and something almost touched fell back out of reach again.

"Don't you think, though, he wouldn't have done it if she weren't doing something wrong? He must have been missing something, surely."

"Oh, I don't know, Edna. Some guys are just pricks that way, and I sure don't know him well enough to say. Anyway, it sounds as if she'll be better off without him. Stella'll do all right, I expect."

I thought he was probably right. And it made her seem far away and different again.

"If you're concerned about her, why don't you write and ask her to stay with us for a while, until she gets organized?"

A pretty picture, two sisters talking. But faced with it, something else. Stella in my home? To have my days disrupted? She would want to talk and talk. I would have to listen. I wanted to talk with her, but not for days. Maybe just for an hour or so.

That wasn't really why, though. The truth was, I didn't want to bring the glowing Stella, and she would still glow — whatever her tragedy she would still be my little dancing sister — into my cool and perfect sanctuary. Harry would see us and wonder. She might make a difference, if he saw us, just the two of us, together, and noticed what I wasn't.

I wanted him to talk about her letter and what we might know of her marriage. I thought it might be an interesting comparison. I thought he might tell me things he didn't otherwise, about how he saw us. I thought if we talked about our marriage, I would know how good it was.

But he wasn't interested. No reason, I guess, why he should have been. He wasn't impatient with my questions, but he wasn't thinking, didn't give thoughtful answers. How was it that he could talk so much about what he cared about, and pay so little attention to something I cared about? Talk to me, Edna, he'd say, but he didn't seem to want me to.

He took up all my listening. I couldn't have had Stella in

the house as well, I could not have listened as much as that.

"Dear Stella," I wrote back. "I'm so sorry. If there's anything I can do, please let me know."

Maybe that's why she does not come to visit.

Later, she wrote to say she wouldn't have time to visit before leaving for Vancouver. "It's all a rush now because we sold the house for the settlement so we could split the money, and now I have my half and no place to live except with Mother and Dad, which is a fate worse than death, so I'm taking off right away."

She found an apartment, sent me her new address. So it was true, this business of an entirely different life was possible.

"Dear Edna, Things are going so well here I can't believe it. It's sort of fun for a change living in a high-rise, where everybody's a stranger and nobody much cares who you are or what you do. Sure different from home! I've walked around and gone to movies and a few bars. I figure I've had my little holiday and now I'm going to salt away the rest of Frank's money (my money, I earned it) and go out looking for a job.

"It drives me crazy to think of all the years I spent missing all this. You can do *anything* here."

"Dear Stella," I wrote. "I'm glad you're settled, and hope you've found a job by now." I would have liked to ask, "What is this pleasure in being able to do anything? How do you choose? Isn't it confusing?" But of course did not.

"Dear Edna, I've landed a pretty good job, working for a bunch of lawyers. Keeping Frank's books and all those commercial courses I took in high school turned out to be a help, so I don't have to start off away down in the typing pool or something. But boy! Living in a big city sure is different. It's a lot harder to get to know people. I guess I'm just too old for some things, too. I mean, I've gone out with a few guys, you can't help meeting men in a lawyer's office, but sometimes it seems so stupid, like being seventeen again, all the hassles. This being single isn't all it's cracked up to be, let me tell you. But on the other hand, it's a change."

So freedom, even for Stella, was not wholly wonderful?

I cleaned a little harder, kissed Harry a little more firmly when he came home from work.

He may not have done or said what I had hoped he would; but there was no question about the need for him. He was all that stood between me and the perilous parts of Stellahood.

A few months later, "Dear Edna, Big news! I've met a perfectly gorgeous man! At least I think he is. His name's Kurt Walther (his folks are German), and he's divorced too, like me, except he's got two kids, but his ex has them. He gets them on weekends, so I do too now; we take them places like the zoo and they seem to be getting used to me. He's an accountant and I met him where I work. (Told you you meet plenty of men in a lawyer's office.) We've been going out pretty regularly for a couple of months now, and I think it's looking good. He's tall and blond and I think he's cute, even if he is going a little bald. He's fun and kind and also smart — all in all, quite a change from Frank!"

And after all that, wasn't it just like Stella, landing on her feet. What did she know about suffering, for her it never lasted. And I wondered just what I meant by that, when I had no suffering at all to do.

Hard to picture her new life. At least before, I'd had a setting for her when I thought of her. Now all the background, where she was and what she did and who this man was, it was just a blur.

They got married, naturally. Stella would not be alone for long. She said in her letter that it was just going to be a quiet civil ceremony and she didn't expect any of us to travel so far to be there. "Maybe some time you'll take a holiday out here and we can get together. Or we'll come east. Let's try, anyway.

"Kurt and I are buying a house, so there'll always be

room for company. He's paying out a lot in alimony and child support, so I'll be keeping on working, at least until his ex remarries which she's showing signs of doing. Anyway, I'd miss working now. I like having my own money and knowing it's there if anything happens. Not that Kurt's anything at all like Frank, but if there's one thing I've learned it's that you never know. Anyway, it makes me feel different to know I can afford to get out if I have to."

I said to Harry, "It sounds like a strange way to go into a marriage. Thinking of getting out again."

"Different, anyway." He sounded so uninvolved and non-committal. "Listen," I wanted to say. "I'm interested in this. I feel strange things, I want to understand what's happened to Stella and what she's done. She's so far away. I listen to you all the time, can't you, for just a little while?" I wanted to bang on the table or his chest, to get his attention.

But of course I wouldn't have wanted him to pretend to be interested if he wasn't. And what exactly was it I wanted to say, or him to tell me? I was beginning to forget.

Later she wrote to say she was pregnant. "Finally," she said. It was a boy. A letter enclosed a picture of her, Kurt, and the baby, named for him. "As you see, both my Kurts are handsome fellows." The photograph was taken with the camera facing into the sun. Stella was holding the baby, and both her face and Kurt's were turned down, looking at the child. There was light around their heads. Kurt's bald spot shone. The background was furry, an impression of green and bushes. She didn't say where it was taken, but by then they'd bought their house, so I suppose it was there. Stella was still slim and still blonde, that much I could see and not much more.

I sent a gift, a little outfit for the baby, with my congratulations. Later when she had a little girl, I did the same. Stella kept working and her children were in day care before they went to school. She became her lawyer's personal assistant. We continued to write letters. Hers were never the same again as that one outburst, that single attempt;

mine were never different from what they'd always been.

Now, in a perverse sort of way, I feel a little free myself.

So I might ask her how it felt to bear a child and how it was to raise one. How it was to start again, to have two men instead of one, to earn a living. How it was to have had the right hair and the right smile and the right words for so long that she could take for granted a leap to the coast of the country, assume she would survive. How she could have all that and the babies, too.

I might ask her why it was she got to start again, and how she knew the way to reach for a second chance and not a knife.

22

PEOPLE STARED.

I remember them, our neighbours, gathered out in the darkness on their lawns, wrapped up in housecoats, wearing slippers, watching, listening. I can hardly blame them. Harry and I would have been out doing the same thing if it had been one of them. If I had not been fully occupied watching the tedious movement of the clock, and then the wallpaper again, and then having all those strange people in my house, I would have been out there watching too.

I would also have been attracted to blood: sign of passion and also of fortune. Because if this happened to someone near, less chance of it happening to oneself. Statistics and odds. It must have cheered our neighbours to have it happen next door, across the street, not in their own living rooms or kitchens.

A lovely day, today. Fresh snow, unmarked. The sun sparkles off it and it looks like jewels, maybe rhinestones, planted across the grounds. Tree branches are stark and still.

For all the missed corners inside, for the moment it is clean and clear and brisk outdoors.

Other places were brisk, but not so clean.

In the first place I went afterward, there were dustballs in the corners, black grime on the windowsills, and untidy heaps of paper on the single big wooden desk. The metal filing trays on it were overflowing. There were two men and a woman in that small cramped room, and me. They kept talking and asking questions and their hands pressed their eyes and foreheads wearily. The sun came up on all their talk and questions.

At home they had told me to change my clothes. So I did; but chose not something special, nothing for an occasion, but another housedress, the kind I did my work in, a small floral print. A dress for my ordinary moments.

All my dresses are here now, and my underwear and robes. Someone must have gone to get them. Someone must have gone into that house.

Oh, but I'm being stupid. A lot of people will have been in and out of that house by now.

Later I was in a small room, still in the same building as the grimy office. The woman there and I had trudged down two flights of stairs from that office to the small room. It had fluorescent lights behind a mesh arrangement in the ceiling, and dull green walls. There were no windows. There was a toilet in a corner, a cot against one wall. I lay down when the woman told me to, and she pulled a scratching grey woollen blanket over me. Was it cold then? It should have been warm, it was July.

It wasn't bad to be there. I was tired, and while the cot sagged and slanted and wasn't like my bed at all, it was a place to lie down. I felt like the colour of the blanket, but not scratchy or rough.

I think I could maybe have just lain there forever, but of course they don't leave you alone. It seems in these circumstances, there is a great deal to be done. The woman came back and made me stand and we walked along a light green corridor, up a different flight of stairs with heavy wooden banisters, along another hallway, this one light-brown-panelled, and into a big room. Like a ballroom or a conference hall, except that it had rows of benches. Like a church, maybe. And like a church a man sitting high up at one end, one had to look up at him. A lot of words were being said.

It wasn't that I could not see or hear. Just that my mind was elsewhere. It seemed to have suspended itself back there a bit, and couldn't get itself here.

I was prepared to wait. The vacuuming wasn't finished, and other things that had to be done hadn't even been started; although the downstairs was as finished as it would ever be. It was a little irritating to be kept away, but I was used to waiting.

It was dark again, which I supposed meant a day gone so I was even further behind, when I was taken to a van outside. The air out there was different from the mustiness inside, but I was only out for a few moments. There was a short ride and then more halls, a different room but with a similar sort of cot, a toilet, and this time, a sink and a chair. They brought trays of food and took them away again. People came and went. Voices went on and on.

The lights did not go out, but I fell asleep. When I woke, I was surprised to find my face damp, tears on my cheeks and soaked into the pillow. I couldn't tell what might have caused that.

Now there were so many rooms, large and small ones, and so many different people and voices and questions, so many places they wanted me to sit and things they wanted me to do. Many men, and a few women. I could feel them: sometimes they were impatient, sometimes angry; but mainly tired, bored perhaps. There was a sense of people sighing all around me.

I could have told them, I suppose. It wouldn't have taken so much effort or concentration. But it was not their business. Harry and I were just the two of us, we always had been. We had no room for strangers. Besides, they were dangerous. They may have been weary and bored, but they also wanted me not to be safe any more. They wanted to put me outside, when I'd been so careful and worked so hard to get inside and stay there where I'd be safe.

I closed my mind against them, folded it over on itself.

More words, more people, more talk, more questions. I came here, to this room. I have only left here once, and that was to go back to one of those big rooms with a man sitting high up at one end. There were a few people watching, scattered along the benches, but I don't think I recognized any of them.

Maybe my parents were there. Or Harry's. Or some of

our friends, or her. But I surely would have recognized them. If I had seen her, I surely would have known.

This was all going on too long. The vacuum cleaner was still lying upstairs in the bedroom, switched off but still plugged in. I hadn't even started on the bathroom. The mirrors would be smudged. I wanted to have it finished.

"Is there anything you'd care to say at this stage, Mrs. Cormick?" the looming man at the end of the room, high up, was asking. He must have been surprised when I spoke up firmly, so they'd all hear and nobody would be able to ignore my wishes.

"I want to go home now, please," I said. "I didn't get the cleaning done."

I know, I understand now, how strange that must have sounded. But it was what was on my mind. It was what I wanted, and when they did take me back out into the sun and we got back into the car, I thought, "Well finally. I should have spoken up before."

But of course the car came right back here.

Oh, I was angry. I was just seething. That night they gave me pills to make me sleep. And where was Harry when I needed him? When he should have helped me, he wasn't there. That I was the cause of his absence, his failure to defend me, was not the point. It was because of him that I was here.

Which was true enough.

If he could fail me, anybody could. The world was once again populated by snapping beasts with their eyes on me.

Never trust. Never relax. Never consider yourself safe. Never speak if it can be helped. Here, especially, words are weapons.

Sometimes, of course, they can't be avoided. When I saw a nurse writing in a notebook just like this one, I had to ask, "Can I have one please?"

She was startled, her head snapped up from her notes.

"What? Did you want something, Mrs. Cormick?"

"Your book. And your pen."

"Oh, well, you can't have this one, I've been using it, but I can see if I can get you one of your own. Would you like that?"

I didn't think she would bring one. Apart from broken promises, they would be leery of pens. But maybe would consider the promise greater than the danger? They would have to weigh that.

It was the doctor, not she, who brought me the first pure, perfect notebook. I don't know what I thought of when I first saw the one in the nurse's hands. A poem maybe. Or some other way to put events in place. Flatten them out with words, or straighten them, or look at them. Or just get rid of them. Put them some place where covers could be shut on them.

They thought a notebook might be an opening? It has built a new wall instead. And this time it is just my wall, I don't have to share it. So no groping fingers are going to poke through this time. In either direction.

This notebook, I can touch it, hold it, it doesn't waver and it has no will of its own, outside of mine. It alters only when I make an alteration in it, in my perfect handwriting.

Often it does not contain what I want it to: which is every small thing here, all written down, identified and pinned. Too often I wander off into the other time. But that is not the notebook's fault, but a failure of my will. Whatever is here, I have made.

Some nights I go to sleep holding it. Not that I mistake it for something else, because it's chilly and smooth. It couldn't possibly be confused with something warm and embracing in return.

But chilly smoothness does not lie; whereas embraces may.

23

EMBRACES MAY LIE. But I admit, some days I miss the illusion.

I may not be able to recall precisely how Harry looked, but I can recall the feel of him. His arm across my body in the night, his shoulder beneath my head. His legs stretched alongside mine. The warmth alone, just that, I miss. I still waken sometimes in the night and turn to the warmth and find it is not there.

I don't remember him as well inside me. That part seems deadened now. There is no stirring or heat in remembering him. There used to be. There used to be something almost sacramental about it. For a few months when I was a young girl, I became religious. Taking communion had a shuddering effect: the bread and the wine that was really grape juice, I would stare at them and try to see in them the actual blood and the body of Christ and shiver at the thought. Harry inside was something like that: sacred in a way, symbolic of the whole, and a link with some unity greater than either of us apart.

I would have liked to consume him in this communion; to draw him whole inside my body, to make us a proper unity. It seemed that must be what he was striving for as well, with all his efforts and strainings.

I suppose he wasn't though. I suppose it must have been something else as far as he was concerned. When the telephone rang, when I found out this was not a sacred act at all, that must be when that part of me lost feeling. Unplugged, another loose end in my body is dangling disconnected.

If Christ came back and said something like, "Oh no, did you think I really meant all those things I said?", people's souls would surely shrivel. Think of all the things that would collapse. And wouldn't the people hate? Wouldn't they kill Christ?

It was not necessarily sacredness I felt at the time, when we were actually together. It was what I felt about the idea of the thing. It was what brought my own passion to our bed.

There were those moments of impending closeness, when I wanted to pull him entirely into my body, all safe and warm the two of us.

But I admit there were other kinds of moments. It isn't always easy to concentrate on what is going on. The mind wanders. One thinks things that are frivolous and unrelated. One thinks, maybe, about being almost out of peanut butter or laundry soap, or what to wear to dinner Saturday. One hears the sounds of making love as sounds, and heard that way they may not be terribly attractive. They may be just slaps of perspiring flesh or short rasping breaths.

And sometimes even odder things occur. I remember that sometimes my mind simply moved away, off into a corner of the room, and my eyes were watching as if I were not a part of it at all; the way I could feel our child watching in those days when we were trying so hard to create him.

From that perspective I saw two strange people on the bed, his familiar buttocks shuddering, legs tensing; and up and down, up and down the body moving. Beneath his heaving outstretched body, I could barely see myself, the second person.

Who would be a voyeur, I wondered, seeing things like this?

Just sometimes this happened — not often, really — and only for a few seconds. Then my eyes would rejoin myself beneath him. I did wonder, though, if this were a flaw or some sort of betrayal.

The best was afterward. Then he had time to be tender

and slow, he would lie close alongside me and stroke my arms, my back. That is what I miss: the tenderness, gentleness, slowness of him all around me.

Then, too, I could draw my fingers along his jaw, examine his cheekbones in the dark, and find his shoulder blades. There was a dent in the small of his back I liked to reach. Beneath the skin was the hardness of his real body. Like a shell around my own soft one. And my own soft body was a dark cubbyhole for him.

It seemed to fit.

I had almost a horror of him holding me in the night and feeling my flesh sag. This can happen easily, with just a little too much weight: lying on your side, your stomach slides towards the mattress and an arm around you feels that, something soft and pliant, like one of those sea animals that don't have any spines. Not a nice thing to feel in the night.

So I did my exercises to stay firm and did not eat too much, and I slept with my back to him or with my head in his shoulder but tilted down, so he wouldn't smell night breath.

I did everything. What didn't I do?

I got used to the idea that there would be no result from all this but blood. No babies. I thought, "Whatever may be missing inside, at least there are no marks. I have stayed firm."

I would not have liked the marks, although I might have liked the babies. I suppose I was like Harry in some ways: wanting everything. "You can't have your cake and eat it too," my mother used to say with some air of weary knowledge. This seemed true.

I also thought, "If we'd had a child, I wouldn't be able to do all this." I meant all the proper care. Instead, there would be playpens, cribs, toys, bottles, boxes of pablum, and jars of green and yellow baby foods, that acid smell of diapers overlaid with sweet baby powder, all the infant aromas of some of the homes we went to. Then tricycles and bicycles and watching and being scared of something terrible happening, a whole new world of fear, having a child.

Just what I did now was complex enough. I might not be equal to two sets of devotion.

Harry said once after a lingering dinner with wine, our private celebration of a promotion I believe, "I'm glad I don't have to share you." I suppose he meant babies.

"Me too."

But surely he could see I wouldn't want to share him either?

We seem to have had different sets of rules. I wish I'd thought to ask what his were.

It's so stupid, such a blindness, not to be able to see him. Twenty years and I see a boy running up behind me on a street, and after that only the sense of a long hard narrow body, a sort of vibration of personality, and a shattering into pieces. Somewhere along the line did I not look?

But we took everything for granted, everything. We never thought.

That house where we lived, that suburb, neat and bleak when we moved in, but after twenty years well treed and flowered — but still neat — it grew up around us. We settled into it like getting comfortable in an easy chair.

We took for granted the big cars traded every other year; the colour television sets as soon as they were on the market; the record player; and later what Harry called the sound system; the very texture of our days.

It's the texture I can feel, not the events. Parties and dinners and conversations and a cup of coffee with a neighbour in a back yard — all these things happened. We had our little disagreements, which hurt, and I did my work. All of it happened in innocence. And all of it is out of focus now, distorted, like a photograph taken from a strange angle with an odd lens, a different perspective entirely. The innocence isn't there in the memory; because the ending casts it in a different light. A mushroom cloud, a blaze of eerie brilliance, twenty years illuminated in a different way that could not have been imagined during the living of them.

At the time, the texture was smooth and soft, like a velvety robe you step into after a bath on a chilly day.

I think I can say with confidence that *we* took it all for granted, that *we* did not think. It must be true for him as well; because if he had thought, if he had not assumed, he could never have dared, could never have risked it, or me, or himself. To take such a leap as he did — well, it can only be done from a trusted, taken-for-granted base.

Unless, of course, he didn't care at all. But he wasn't such a liar as that. He lied, but not like that.

He must have changed, though, in other ways than new glasses and stooping shoulders. I aged and changed, whatever my efforts, and of course he must have too. Grey hairs, lines, a dragging of the skin, these things must have happened to him as well.

If I failed to see all that, what about invisible changes?

Is that what he thought, that I failed to see him? Did he just want somebody to look?

It could as easily be the reverse, for all I know. He might have thought I saw too well, or too much, and wanted a little time to be invisible.

It wasn't so much time. A small portion of our years.

When I lie in bed looking up, what I see are white ceiling tiles. I've counted the holes in them, which is not an easy thing to do. You get a certain way along and the holes blur and two of them seem to jump together and you have to start again. But by going slowly and patiently along the lines, I have counted twenty-three along each side. Each corner hole, of course, is counted twice, once for each of the two sides it connects.

With such exercises I refine myself.

When I brush my teeth, I draw an inch of toothpaste along the bristles. On a bad day, when someone else brushes my teeth, a little less is likely to be used. I brush before and after breakfast, and then not until bedtime. I used to smoke occasionally, but here they don't permit matches; so my breath, I imagine, is better and there's no great need to brush during the day. Is an inch of toothpaste every time wasteful? Or countered by only brushing three times a day?

Harry said, "You look great." Or "How about the red dress Friday?" But he might have preferred me to have scars or birthmarks or wear more make-up or dress differently. He might have liked a change.

Sometimes he said, "Edna, are you okay?" and I didn't know what he meant. "I mean," he'd say, "you just stay home. Are you okay?" and he'd have a worried, puzzled look.

Did he not want me to vacuum every day or wipe the toaster? Did he want me to be the life of all the parties? People still complimented him, he told me, on his small dark quiet listening wife. I couldn't be everything. He embraced the person I was, and yet there were those times when the person I was seemed to concern him.

But he wouldn't have liked to have no clean shirts, or to see dirty dishes in the sink.

So just what did he want, anyway? What more did he want?

There are so many interruptions here. That's a hard thing to get used to, after so many years of privacy.

They come in and say, "Come on now, it's time for breakfast." Or lunch, or dinner. "Okay, Edna, let's have your bath now." And "Time to go see the doctor," which is one I don't mind so much, although it's sometimes inconvenient, sometimes I am in the middle of something here.

"Lights out, Edna," they say at night. "Time to put the pen down now."

It's tiring, all this work, all this writing, all this picking apart of things. They only give me sleeping pills on the bad days. Otherwise I sleep quite well, except for waking up sometimes in the middle of the night and reaching for the missing warm part. All my habits have been broken here, except for that one drowsy one.

At the end of a day my eyes burn, and my right wrist,

my fingers, feel all cramped and sore from the steady, tidy writing.

But it makes me uneasy to have the lights out, to go to sleep. I can't write in the dark, so maybe I miss things? With the pen I might be able to follow falling asleep, for instance, to see how that happens.

Other times, too, the pen and the notebook are inaccessible. At meals they don't let me have them and it's hard to write the details from memory, hard to pay enough attention to remember adequately. How exactly it feels, moving a spoon to the mouth.

And in the bath, another place I can't take the notebook, may there not be some sensation of water and soap and skin forgotten?

There are so many things to put down. Right here in this chair there are so many things. And then I drift off and write down other things as well. I still do not pay attention well enough. But I see a good deal better than I used to. I'm developing a better eye for detail than I ever had before.

24

I USED TO WONDER SOMETIMES why people like Harry were given holidays. Like money, I suppose, they represent reward, accomplishment. In the early days of our marriage we'd not had a great deal of money, but enough, and a couple of weeks' vacation was not much but enough. Then, as the years went on, we had more and more money, more than enough, and the weeks of holiday expanded too and were also much more than enough.

Vacations are for doing. One is supposed to see new things, rest, and break patterns, and return refreshed to ordinary labours. But what is it one is supposed to do?

Go away, travel, leave home. But home was where my life was; leaving there, to drive across the country or to fly to Florida or California or some Caribbean island was to be nowhere at all. We ate different kinds of fruit and drank different kinds of drinks. We stayed in hotels where other people, maids, changed the sheets and cleaned the toilets and where there was likely a view of a beach from the balcony. We could rent cars to drive along rutted roads, or read books beside a hotel pool, stretched out on lounge chairs in our bathing suits and sunglasses. We could walk along sand at sunset. We could look like pictures on a travel poster.

But my hands were empty when we were away. They missed what they should be doing. They missed holding dishcloths and food. They lacked purpose, and didn't know what to do with themselves.

Harry, too, may have felt that, because his fingers sometimes drummed on tables while we waited for drinks, and he would break into a run along a beach, leaving me behind, and at night would fling himself onto a hotel bed and sometimes sigh. He would wonder what was happening with some deal at the office, or how he ought to solve some problem. A holiday often seemed to be empty time, an uncomfortable pause.

We went together to Jamaica, Barbados, St. Lucia, Hawaii. Once we went to Mexico, and another time, daringly, on a package tour to Cuba, which we thought would be a stern and exotic place. But it did not seem so different. From hotels and beaches, the view is much the same.

We went to California and walked different kinds of streets and beaches and stared around for movie stars. And Florida. It was heat and water that attracted us, the antidote to winter cold and grey and snow. Like birds, we migrated south.

We drove, in summers, through New England and northern Ontario and to both coasts, planning itineraries, drawing lines on maps, scanning guides for good hotels. Mainly we were not drawn to big cities, although in the spring or fall Harry might take some extra days and we'd fly to New York, stay in some safe hotel, and journey out to dinner and the theatre. We did not walk there, of course. The dangers were too well known. North America in general seemed too familiar, because we were alert to what could happen. What could happen in other places, we could not be sure, so travelled there more freely.

It was nice to see the plays. In the dark, except for the coughing and some murmuring, it was almost private, like watching a drama from our living room. And in the dark I could see myself up on the stage.

They also gave us conversation. We could go back to our room and put up our feet and order from room service and talk about performances. When we got home, Harry liked telling people what we'd seen and done. The luxury of being able to do these things, fly to New York for a four-day weekend, appealed to both of us.

(Did she miss him when we went away? Did he miss her? There were meetings Harry went to out of town. Did she go with him, were those their holidays?)

We did not always go away though. Sometimes Harry took a week or two and stayed home, puttering around the house. He put in gardens and painted rooms and once sanded down a table and refinished it. Every day or so he'd call his office, or someone from there would call him, which both pleased him and kept his mind on work, which seemed to make him both more tense and more content.

Those holidays at home were odd for me, too. He came into the kitchen wanting a sandwich or a beer and it was midday, when he shouldn't have been there at all. Sounds were disorienting — coughs and hammering, footsteps and his voice, when normally there would be silence. My treats were deferred. Certainly I could not put on records in the afternoon, lie down on the couch, close my eyes, and dance.

I could feel his body tightening as it came time to go back to work. On the morning of the first day back, he would be chattering and laughing, and he grinned back at me as he went out the door.

I did not grin, was not exactly happy; but closed the door behind him with some sense of peace restored.

The trouble when we went away was the tension of words between us. We spoke of what we saw and did, but had little other conversation. Even Harry, without his work, was a bit bereft of words. We said, "Look at that sunset," and "Shall we drive around the island tomorrow?" and "Did you ever see anything like what that woman is wearing!"

What do other people talk about? Maybe much the same, except that they don't notice, or it's enough, or it doesn't seem important.

Maybe it was that we didn't belong where we went, and knew that these places were only a space in our time, that endings were coming up. Surely, though, that would be the same for anyone on holiday? A vacation is mainly observation, there is no settling in. Our own lives were not led in sunshine or on sandy beaches, or even in the hotels that might have been anywhere. We watched the natives, the tanned Californians and the brown Caribbeans, but knew less of them than we would have watching television. It was somewhat like watching television, and even seemed as if we had already seen much of it and were still watching from behind a screen. We were fish out of our own waters and not sufficiently relaxed.

And too, not having children made a difference. Holidays must be so simple, if also perhaps more aggravating, for people with children. Then, there are always things to do and places to see. One goes, no doubt, to Disneyland instead of for a walk. A wax museum instead of a long dinner heavy with drinks. Children must provide some form to these things and a familiar structure. The vital part of home travelling right along with you, making its homelike demands. Harry and I never went to Disneyland or to wax museums. They were hardly to our tastes.

Maybe we should have talked about it; discussed our discomfort at having so little to discuss. Maybe we should have said, "Gosh, three weeks together is really a long time, isn't it?"

Instead, we touched a great deal more than usual, and made love more often. We reassured each other with our bodies.

There was never a lack of fondness between us; just that there were limited ways of telling our fondness. And with only the two of us for days and days, this was drawn to our attention.

But when I viewed us as a picture, if I observed us as some other person might, Harry's arm around me when we walked, or bent together over a map on the hood of our rented car, or lying side by side tanning by a pool, reading bits of books or papers to each other — it was a charming picture. We looked so happy.

We were happy. It was only odd, that's all.

In my head I counted off the days until we would be going home. And Harry, also aware of diminishing moments, said things like, "We only have six days left, we should try to hit the market tomorrow, time's running out." The night before we left wherever we had gone, we achieved some gaiety, laughed easily and drank more and talked eagerly about the holiday now gone. In those nights of retrospect, the time away could safely glitter.

When we came home, drove up that street and in that driveway, when I saw our ordinary house, I could have embraced it. Put my arms around it and kissed its doors and windows. As soon as Harry went back to work, I set about making it fresh and clean again, because in our absence it would have become a bit unused-smelling; not quite musty, but not quite familiar or ours. I did not like it that when we walked out the door, the house could forget us and set about gathering dust and different smells.

Our holidays felt strange, but not disastrous. Unless muteness is a tragedy. But beforehand we were not mute, and I think our true vacations were in the planning of them. Each year we looked ahead as if the weeks away would be perfect, and were as entertained and as excited as the vacations themselves were probably meant to make us.

"I've got six weeks this year," Harry said. "What do you think we should do with them?"

And we would talk about places maybe read about or for which there'd been advertisements on television, where we had already been, and if new places would be much different. Harry would go to travel agents (or send her out to them?) and bring home brochures and schedules of flights and lists of prices. We would stare at the pictures of high-rise hotels and judge their proximity to beaches and imagine ourselves in one of the rooms, standing at one of the tiny windows in the photographs.

People at work told Harry about their holidays, which islands in the Caribbean might be unpleasant this year, with relations strained between natives and tourists, or dangerous, or too dull. For people who wanted more than tans, who liked to keep busy, as we did, some places should be avoided. The Caribbean seemed the natural area to go to, however. There were formulas for the islands, one knew more or less what to expect, and yet they were quite different from home. We hugged ourselves in December, contemplating February on a beach, or buying shirts and straw hats in a market.

"I can't wait," Harry would say. "I can't wait to get away from that damned office."

Our enthusiasm beforehand never faltered.

Like children, we stared out airplane windows and pointed down, excited, at the clouds.

I was only frightened taking off and landing.

In the little buses that took us to our hotels we looked out windows and judged how interesting this place might be.

I think it was not until we were checked in, unpacking in our room, and just the two of us, that the weariness set in.

I would, I think, have liked to go to Europe. To see castles in Britain and old wineries in France. In Spain, we could even have lain on beaches. But the time of year was never right, it was harder to count on sunshine. And Harry said, "It's all old there, it's dying. They've only got the past. Who wants to go trailing through museums and old ruins? Nothing's *moving* over there." He said it would be boring, and they were his holidays after all, he earned them, and it was he who needed the rest, the break, the change of pace.

Now, though, if I could travel, that's where I'd go. To cool places: Scotland in autumn, even if it rained, or the mountains in Spain in the spring. I would walk by myself through big cities like Paris and stare at all the old things: buildings and paintings and monuments. I don't think those things are dying at all. I think I would be reassured to see that some things do survive centuries, they last. Unlike snow or leaves or houses or days.

Or that there have been so many people and events in so many years — the past is huge — that two people in a moment now have no great significance. They may be something only tiny, and all this very little, really.

25

"TALK TO ME, EDNA," he said, although not, I admit, so often in the last few years. It would not be fair to say he didn't pay attention. (Strange to worry about being fair, which would seem the least of it.)

"Are you all right?" he asked. "Are you okay home alone like this?" What did he think was happening?

Maybe if something was happening to him, he needed to search out some strangeness in me.

He began to leave for work earlier in the mornings because, he said, "I beat the worst of the traffic this way. I wish I'd thought of it before." I still woke him gently; just earlier.

It meant going to bed at nights earlier, so our evenings together were shorter.

They were also shorter because he began often to come home later, too. Again, he said, avoiding the rush hour. Or working late. Sometimes he stayed downtown overnight. "It's this damn job," he told me, and of course he had been promoted again, to manager of marketing, so it was reasonable to imagine him working still harder. She was promoted along with him. He told me and laughed because he said it was called rug-ranking, and wasn't that an odd expression.

We still had most of our evenings, though, even if they became briefer. And our weekends, we had those. There were only small incursions into our time, so subtle and so reasonable. "Of course," I said. "I understand." And thought I did.

I leaped and slid past thirty to forty. It went so fast;

oddly, because each day was long and full of hours.

Forty. I woke up the morning of that birthday and remembered it was that day and felt the oddest sense of doom. It was, and this was rare, really, hard to get out of bed.

I seem to have had common crises. It must be just that I never learned to deal with them in common ways, that's it, I guess.

Really a birthday is just a number. But to shift a decade and not merely a year is something; although I imagine the next move, into fifties, won't be so much now. I lack a sense of future.

Hormones, possibly. My doctor once said shifting moods could usually be traced to shifting hormones. It gave me a particularly helpless feeling: that nothing, it seemed, not even a mood, was just my own.

But that morning, my birthday, was more than hormones. They may have sunk, but everything else was dragged down also.

Because there ought to be a clear view here. A little peak from which one can look back and see forty years in a bundle and look forward and see how it will go and the clarity alone should be satisfying. One ought to have things in place. One ought to be able to say, "I have done that," and "I will do this." There should be something like an A on a report card, even a B would be satisfactory. What about Harry? He would, I suppose, have his promotions and his pay cheques. A steady progress; piles of accomplishments like steps behind him.

But for me? If one does the same thing over and over again, each time properly, each time to the best of one's ability, still what one seems to have is a handful of endless identical tasks. It's not like getting anywhere.

There was a purpose, of course. I had my reasons. Just that on this day the vision slipped. Instead of the larger purpose, I saw the tiny tasks. They crowded my head, jumbling into each other, a tumbling of dishes and laundry and dusting and scrubbing and exercises and make-up, of watching the clock to see when Harry would be home. And the second, secret closed-eyed life of being someone else up on a stage, and all the music. In this fortieth birthday light, all that was absurd and sad, and I thought I might not now be able to return to it, having seen it this way.

I stood stock still in the kitchen, a frying pan in one hand, an egg in the other, struck with a thought, not a blow: "This is nothing. This is not anything at all."

Imagine such a thought on a fortieth birthday: no wonder I had to stand still, breathless for a moment.

None the less, the egg had to be cracked into the frying pan, the toast had to be made, the juice poured, the coffee percolated.

Every move like being on a planet where the gravity is enormous: the limbs weighed down, dragging to the earth. I might just sink, standing there, through the kitchen floor.

And there was Harry, sitting across the table from me, the smells the same as any morning, the sun streaking light across the kitchen table, and it was like every morning of my life; except that the smells were sour and I was dark. The coffee was bitter and my cigarette was dust in my lungs. Small pleasures were only small, after all.

I sighed and heard my mother sighing. Was this what happened?

"Happy birthday," Harry said. "But you look as if it's bugging you." See, I remember that, that he did know, he did pay attention, it was me sitting there across from him, living with him, he did know that.

It's hard not to come fiercely to his defence, even against myself. It's difficult to break a habit of more than twenty years. And it's confusing to remind myself that he also lied, and that there was a time when he needed defending and I was unavailable.

Some time, oh years ago, in the early days of being married, he'd come home from work and we'd have dinner and when it got to be dusk and then dark we'd turn out all the lights and put records on the player and kick off our shoes and dance together in the dark. Snuggled close we'd drift around the living room, eyes closed, to gentle songs. The Mills Brothers harmonized, "You always hurt the one you love." But we moved to the rhythms, not the words. And who really listens to songs? Who takes them as far as they'll go?

I can't quite recall when we stopped doing that. Like other things, some of our hours together, they must have just drifted off and we forgot.

I hadn't realized how many shiftings there were.

"You sure don't look forty," Harry was saying. Even a compliment turned on itself. What did forty look like? One of these days would I crumble, my true and forty-year-old face appearing abruptly, irreversibly aged? Some day nothing, not all the exercises or all the creams and lotions and care, would make a difference. I knew, although he may not have noticed, that there were already little lines, tiny baggings at the base of my throat. I bought scarves, which I never had before, to hide them. This was just the beginning; the force of earth would work its way down my breasts, my stomach, and my thighs.

Maybe it shouldn't make a difference. But it does. To slide into age without ever having seen yourself, and after so much effort. All the time is gone.

Forty years gone. Into an even division of fear and safety, twenty years of this, another twenty of that. And another twenty, forty years? Oh God, the weariness, the weight, of all those years of endless little tasks. Was Harry big enough?

Ah, but there was a dangerous, betraying thought. Question that and anything might happen; I might shatter into pieces just sitting in my chair.

"Really, Edna," and I shook myself. "Whatever is the matter? Pull yourself together," and I tried, made an effort to haul back the wandering, desolate, betraying, destroying thoughts.

It certainly wasn't any longing for change. The very thought of change would terrify me. So what was it I wanted?

Just a little while to get used to the idea. Of being forty, in my forties, of catching up to it. Just a little time.

"Are you sick or something? You look pale." He'd put down his fork, his diagonal slice of buttered toast, his cup of coffee. He was just looking at me. What did he see? I felt my fingers around my throat, hiding lines. I would have put my hands over my face.

"No, I'm fine."

"Christ, Edna, if it's just your birthday, it's not a tragedy, you know. You don't have to look as if it's the end of the world. I'm older than you and look at me, am I over the hill?"

Yes, as it happens.

"Of course not. I'm just being silly. It's hit me funny, that's all. Remember your fortieth birthday, it bothered you too, you know." And it had. I'd baked a cake and given him my gift at dinner, an incredibly expensive pair of gold cuff links engraved with his initials, but he was so quiet. He drank steadily, almost sullenly, through the evening and went to bed drunk. "Thank you for the cuff links," he said. "They're nice." He hardly ever got drunk.

"Shit, it's nothing. You don't look anything like forty." And there it was again. What would he say, then, when I did?

"Listen," and he grabbed my hands across the table. My hands that were not so soft or unused any more. "Tell you what. Grab a cab down to the office at five and we'll go out for drinks and dinner. You should be celebrating, not feeling bad. We'll have a great meal and a few bottles of wine and you can spend the day treating yourself and getting ready. Just lie around in the tub with some really whiffy bath oil. Doll yourself up, look good tonight. And I'll show you how much fun being forty can be." He leered, and we laughed. Maybe it was not so terrible. Maybe small pleasures were small miracles, and not just small.

"Okay. You're right. That'll be nice." But did he think a few words and a grin, a long bath and an expensive dinner would lift wrinkles, flesh, time?

A day off might lead to other days: to anarchy. I worked through the morning, as I always did. This was hard and heavy work, not so little. But grim today; I could not quite make out salvation in the unsmudged glass of mirrors.

In the aftertoon I had the long hot bath with the expensive oil, lay in the tub with my cigarettes and magazines, then did my hair. I would wear my blue silk suit, elegant and lean. How would a woman of forty dress? I looked at my clothes and most of them seemed ageless; but one would have to study what was suitable.

I was well turned out when I left, if not beautiful. But this was following his instructions; not a treat, as he'd intended, but another small thing that must be done.

I was impatient at my unfairness and lack of gratitude. What did I want, anyway? Just to be told it was important, maybe.

In his office, before we left, he handed me a yellow rose, clipped the stem, and hooked it into the buttonhole of my suit, stepped back, head cocked, surveying. "You look great," he said, and kissed my cheek. (And this, I remember, in front of her. Had he no shame, for either of us?

(Surely I was real to them. Surely I was not so invisible that they didn't notice me; that he might even have sent her out to buy the rose? Would that be part of her job? The possibilities of these little things, tiny wounds, are almost as painful and betraying as the great one.)

I said to him once, "I think a single rose is better than a dozen big ones. Anybody can give a bunch of flowers, but just one is special." I was touched that he remembered.

"Happy birthday, Edna," he said in the restaurant, lifting his glass of white wine to me. "To you, my perfect wife."

Extravagant? Oh yes, Harry was extravagant in his speech as well as in other ways. What did he mean by perfect? That I was deaf and dumb and blind and stupid?

A smile, a rose — these should be good returns on my investment.

"So," he said, "Are you feeling better? Did you do what I said and pamper yourself today?"

See, questions. An evening of questions. But he was interested. He wasn't talking about himself. It was my fault that I couldn't think what to tell him, or what to ask.

Years of listening, droplets of facts plinking into the well of my mind, opinions splashing down. But always he said something just to me: asked about my day, or what I was doing or planning to do, what I was reading. and what I felt like seeing on television. He always gave me a chance to take a turn, so it must have been my fault when I didn't. Maybe he only talked to fill my gaps? But no, that's going too far. He talked because he wanted to tell me things; or to hear himself telling me things.

"Yes, I'm feeling better." My fingers kept going to the rose, to see if it was enough. "It was just this morning, it struck me strange. To think of being in my forties, you know. As if everything's been — so short." I may have meant so small. How was he to know?

"Well," and he grinned at me, "you're not dying, you know."

But of course that's part of it. Forty says precisely that you're dying, you can almost glimpse it, that this is going to end and you will lie at that end on a great heap of very small pieces of this and that.

"Is it because you feel you've missed things? Are there things you wanted to do and couldn't?"

He knew better than that. We went over all that before we were even married. He knew perfectly well I had no ambitions.

"Of course not. It's just something to get used to." I shrugged. "It's not a big deal, it's just silliness, I told you."

We were eating, but he kept glancing at me, peering as if he wanted to see past my skin. My skin that didn't look forty yet.

"All I ever wanted was to make a good home."

"And you've done that right enough," he said, lifting his glass again to me and drinking. Did he wonder at my ambition? Did he feel worthy of it, or ashamed?

"Don't you think that's enough?" In a moment I would cry, and wouldn't quite know why.

"Of course it is, if that's what you want. All I was asking was if there was anything else you wanted and didn't get."

Somehow there was an edge in both our voices. What edge were we close to? Should we have stepped over instead of back?

"Harry, it's just realizing I'm not seventeen, I'm forty, and this is what I'm doing, this is it. Do you see?"

And blessedly he did see, here was the step away from the brink. "Yeah, actually I think I do. You wonder how it happened, what happened, it goes so fast."

"Exactly." I beamed and thought, "We are close."

"Well, of course I wanted a child, maybe. For a while." To bring this up, that is how close I thought we were right then. Was that so rare then? So it would seem; it would seem almost as if our minds must have run for years on parallels, quite separate, and would have done so to infinity.

"Do you think about it much?"

"No, hardly ever any more. Just that when you asked if there was anything I wanted and didn't get, well, that's what you'd think of too, isn't it?"

"I guess. It would have been different, wouldn't it?"

"Hard to imagine now."

Now I could feel the evening draining. Difficult and tiring to keep up with abrupt shiftings, from the undercurrent of hostility to the closeness, from his questions to my uneasy confusion, and now to a kind of minor gloom for our lost lives, lost children, whatever we might have mourned if we'd been people who mourned for things that were impossible. Which we weren't, at the time.

What if I'd turned his questions back? If I'd said, "What

about you? What do you feel you've missed? Have you done what you wanted? Are you satisfied? With me? And everything else? What more do you want?"

Who knows what he might have told me, with a candle on the table and wine in our glasses and a rose in the buttonhole of my blue silk suit? He might have said he was unhappy and dissatisfied, that he was worried, or frail, or that he wanted a great deal more. He might have said the truth, whatever that was. We might both have said the truth.

But what then? Might I not have reached out and plunged my steak knife publicly into our little tragedy?

A little tragedy, yes. Nothing unique, no headlines, I'm sure. I wonder if it was even in the papers? Just a simple, ordinary, domestic failure.

But he was grinning, and just like at breakfast reached across the table for my hands, held them, covered them. "That's enough of that sad shit. We're supposed to be celebrating. You've earned forty years, you should be proud. You've got forty years under your belt."

But when would they start to sag?

"You're just halfway, really. Come on, let's drink to our eightieth birthdays and our sixtieth anniversary."

And of course I laughed with him. His laughter was still infectious; and besides, it was a funny vision, the two of us old and lined and bent and still — always — together. It was not the old that was discouraging but the years it took to get there.

"To us," he said. "May you be as beautiful and I be as handsome then as we are today."

But I was not beautiful. He was handsome, but I was not beautiful. What did he see?

"Do you think my hair's getting too grey? Should I start touching it up?"

"Hell no. It suits you, it's kind of warm and soft like you. Besides, there isn't much. And anyway, it's like being forty, it's something you've earned. You should be proud."

I don't think he really believed that. He was just trying

to cheer me up, which was kind. But what did I do to earn forty years and grey hairs? I don't think I'm vain; just frightened. Or is it the same thing?

"Why fight it? Why hide what you are?"

Habit, I guess. Necessity.

"It's a waste of time to get upset about things you can't do anything about."

I hope he meant that. I hope he really believed it, and was not upset in the end by what he could not prevent.

"But listen, apart from today and having a birthday, are you happy? Are you okay?"

Okay, certainly. Apart from today and a birthday. Happy? It's funny. When you're young, maybe you think about being happy. I used to hope for that, and if somebody'd asked me, "What do you want to be?" I might have said, "Happy," and I would have thought that meant just one thing.

But you forget. If you're like me and get what you thought was going to make you happy, the idea of it kind of fades. I supposed I should be happy. I supposed I was. But it didn't seem quite the word.

What would the word be? Content, by and large? Satisfied? But both implied a sitting back, a relaxing, a serenity, and that was not much like my days in which so much had to be accomplished.

"I'm busy," I said slowly. I could tell by his face, a bit startled, disappointed, that that was neither right nor enough. "I'm happy, naturally. How couldn't I be?"

"I don't know. You never say. You never say how you feel."

"Well, there's no need, is there? I feel fine. My life is just the way I wanted it to be." My God, there was a desolation in that sentence I didn't intend at all.

"Look, Edna," and he was looking at me so firmly, as if I were some recalcitrant employee, and he sounded almost angry; what did he want from me? "Look, you were upset this morning about being forty. I understand that, it can hit anybody that way. But I worry about you sometimes. I don't know what your days are like and how you feel about them and what you think about. The house is great, and of course you've made it a place to be proud of." (But it hadn't been pride I was hoping for; it was refuge.) "But what else?"

What did he mean, what else? "What are you worried about?"

"Your days. How you spend them."

"Harry, you know what my days are like. For heaven's sake!"

"No, I don't. I can see what you do, if that's what you mean, but I still don't know how they feel."

I shrugged. "They feel busy. I don't understand what you want, Harry."

"I want to know," and he looked so fierce and harsh I could almost have been frightened, "if it's really enough for you to look after a house and me." But he softened. "I just want to know if you're okay. Because you've been doing it all for twenty years, and sometimes I think you must get bored. Don't you? Don't you sometimes want to try different things?"

Bored sometimes, yes. But that is surely to be expected; part of the trade for a life.

"Well, different days feel different, they're not the same. Sometimes I get tired and sometimes I enjoy it. It's like anybody else, I expect. Don't you ever get down at work, or tired of it? After all, Harry, I don't know how it feels to be you doing what you do all day any more than you know about me and my days."

"Well, you should," and he was smiling again, thank God. "I tell you enough about it. Sometimes I wonder how you can listen to so much of it."

So should I have told him that sometimes it was difficult and dull to listen and that I could never feel it had anything much to do with me?

"No, I like to hear about your days."

Who am I to call him a liar?

What did they talk about? Did they discuss everything,

did she speak easily, and then did he miss the same kind of thing with me? Did they talk about me? That night in the restaurant in this strange tense conversation on my birthday, how much was he comparing us?

Oh, I could kill him.

Maybe what I lack is a better sense of humour.

"Look, Harry, let's just drink the wine and enjoy the evening. I'm forty, okay? I'm fine."

Usually I couldn't drink so much wine. Usually it made me sleepy. But tonight it seemed I could have gone on drinking it forever and it would have soaked right into my body and not left a trace, no wobbling or slurring or sleepiness or even having to go to the bathroom. I seemed to be working it off, like sweat, in talk and uneasiness.

"But don't you get lonesome, Edna? I mean there you are in that house and a lot of times I don't get home for dinner now. Don't you want to get out sometimes and see other people? Don't you get mad?"

"Well, I see neighbours. We have coffee sometimes. But I don't get lonely. I like being by myself, I always have. I get a lot of work done, and I like to read. I like to make the house clean, it's peaceful in a way, making things shine. And I like sitting in the kitchen at four o'clock having a coffee and thinking about you coming home."

"But what about when I'm not coming home? What if I'm going to be late or not make it at all?"

"That's okay. I watch TV and read, or sometimes I bake if there hasn't been time during the day. There are things to do. Of course I'd like it better if you came home, but I can find things to do."

"And you don't get mad?"

"Heavens, no. Why should I?"

Why indeed.

Anyway, we made a bargain: I would not make demands, and he would give. But what was he giving? Never mind. Twenty years down the road was no time to tell him I was waiting.

Oh, wasn't I the perfect, understanding wife though?

Once, Harry brought home a man from work for a drink. They sat in the living room talking, while I tried to keep dinner from being ruined. I imagine the man's wife was trying to do the same in their home. After a couple of hours the man stood and sighed and said, "Well, I better be getting home to the old ball and chain."

What an ugly thing to say, a terrible way to feel. "It's just an expression," Harry told me later. But expressions don't come from nowhere, and that man said that so easily, casually, about his wife. Not Harry. Not ever Harry.

"So what you're saying is that you're quite happy and contented and everything is tickety-boo, is that right?" A cynicism, bitterness, in the tone; so odd. And how do you answer?

"I suppose. If you want to put it that way. Harry, please let's just drop it. I'm perfectly satisfied with my life."

He flung up his hands. "Okay, okay. If you're sure. I just wanted to be sure."

I guess he really wasn't asking about me at all that night. I guess he was really checking for permission to be free.

At home we just got in the door and he said, "I'm beat, I'm going to bed. Happy birthday, Edna." I'd thought we might sit up for another glass of wine; and cool down from the evening and whatever was hot (and not warm) between us. But he did look weary.

I was restless still and stayed downstairs for a while, looking around. Just wandering through the rooms, staring at shining surfaces. Like my clothes: would my furniture suit my age? I approved the starkness of Rosenthal vases in the dining room and the cool beige woven couch in the living room, the simple silver frame on a mildly modern print of something not quite like what it was. I liked the smooth surfaces and the textured ones. So cool and light, my rooms.

But were they for a forty-year-old woman? Or did that matter, as long as they were tasteful. Magazines instructed in taste, and in changing tastes, changing just as the rules seemed to. I had no need for new rules, though, having embraced my own. And no need to alter simplicity for old flowery cake plates and painted vases, rough wooden tables instead of glass and chrome, heavy patterned furniture instead of light and plain. These new things were old, would have more nearly suited my parents' home than mine. Things — tastes and rules — seemed to be going backward and forward simultaneously. Very confusing.

Probably having learned simplicity so well, I should stick to it. At forty, surely one has a right to say, "This is it." Even if along with the satisfaction of saying that comes just a hint of death.

The daisy kitchen clock moved on past midnight, and I was into my forty-first year.

Harry was sound asleep when I went upstairs. I looked at him and wondered, "What were all those questions for? Why did he want to stir things up?" But what had he stirred up? I tossed for a while before I got to sleep.

But was up early the next morning, the morning of the first day of my forty-first year, and couldn't quite recall the day before. It seemed an aberration. What had seemed so hard, or bad? Too many questions; and with too many questions a faltering of purpose, a betrayal. A relief to settle back on my own track.

It seemed important to demonstrate to Harry that I was fine. He needn't worry, or even think about me. Things were as they should be, and he could go unburdened to his office. Certainly I did not want him to look at me again in quite the way he had the night before, or talk to me that way again.

Pancakes were usually for weekends when there was lots of time and lots to do; but I made pancakes that morning anyway, for proof.

"Very nice," he said, and ate four. No questions this morning, no signs of the night before. "I've got to run if I want to beat the rush. See you later. I think I should be home for dinner, I'll let you know."

I waved good-bye and started my work. I would not think of twenty, forty years, enough to take each day.

I forgot how sad the closed-eyed music had seemed the day before, and put on an album in the afternoon, watched myself whirl on a stage, and smiled.

Later, he called to say he wouldn't be able to make it for dinner after all, but should be home by nine. "Listen, Edna," and he laughed, "don't ever make pancakes again on a weekday."

"Why not?"

"I've got a gut you wouldn't believe. Weighs a ton. I can hardly move. All I want to do is sleep."

"I'm sorry. I didn't think of that."

"Shit, I was kidding." So easily he twisted on me in recent years; and again I didn't really notice. "They were great, it's just when you sit on your ass all day, it's hard to work them off. If I was home mowing the lawn, they'd be gone by now. Listen, I've got to get to a meeting. See you later, okay?"

So. Dinner for one. An omelette and a small salad in front of the television set; another meal without Harry, another meal at which I could watch my weight. I watched Walter Cronkite while I ate. Who was Walter Cronkite anyway? Did he have secrets, tell lies? It didn't seem so, but the faces, it seems, are just masks for other faces.

Was I like that as well? Or was my flaw maybe just transparency?

26

THE PHONE CALL FROM THAT WOMAN; Dottie Franklin. Why would she do such a thing? One assumes malice. Maybe I deserved malice.

I knew her, of course. We'd had dinners, the four of us, she and Jack, Harry and I, and we also met at parties. The first time, years ago, before I met them Harry told me a little about them. He always tried to do that, give me details about people we were seeing, so I'd feel more a part of it, I suppose, or not say something wrong, or so they wouldn't seem quite like strangers.

"Don't, for God's sake, talk about marriage," he told me. Why ever would I have raised such an intimate subject anyway? But he was warning, "It's a bad topic, especially if they have a few drinks." Everyone always had a few drinks.

"Why?"

"Because theirs is weird and if you get them started, it'll all turn into a brawl."

"But what's the matter?"

"Who knows?" He raised his eyebrows, spread his palms towards me, shrugged. "Probably a lot of things. The obvious one is that Jack's a bit of a chaser, and every year or so he takes up with somebody for a while until he does something stupid, I don't know, goes home with blonde hairs on his jacket maybe, and Dottie finds out. Then they have a hell of a row and heave things around and then they make up, sort of, until the next time."

"But that's terrible. Why do they stay together if it's so awful?" Astonished that people might yell and throw dishes and live in the midst of betrayal.

"Probably because they like it that way. It's never one person's fault, you know." No, I don't suppose it is. "Jack's not such a bad guy, it's just the way he is. And in their way, they get along. Maybe they like fighting, maybe they get off on it."

And when we met them, it did seem they got along. Jack wasn't sharp and bright, not like Harry, but he did have an easy sort of charm, I could see his type. He might be attractive, if one were inclined to casualness.

And he and Dottie had little married jokes, small verbal nudges, and grinned at each other, and if there was a hard sort of undercurrent, maybe I only heard it because I knew to listen for it.

"We were lucky," Harry said afterward. "They weren't too bad tonight."

I remember looking at her, though, and feeling sorry for her. And I must confess a straightening of my spine, a pride that Harry and I were different.

If she phoned out of malice, that's understandable.

But unforgivable if it was done with pity. If it was true that she thought it only "fair" to tell me. If, as she lifted the receiver, dialled, she thought, "Poor Edna."

"It was just by accident Jack saw them," she told me. "He happened to glance out the car window as he was going past her apartment building and there they were in the parking lot. Kissing.

"And after all, at eight o'clock in the morning, what other explanation could there be?

"I thought you ought to know. I thought it would be only fair."

One thing I thought during my twelve long hours of thinking, fixed on that wall of gold-flecked white wallpaper: that the unique, flamboyant, clever, driving Harry, who hadn't made it home last night, could have committed such an ordinary, clichéd, banal little sin. That he could have been trapped in one of my magazine articles, that is how ordinary he turned out to be, and that was a betrayal, too.

If he were going to do such a thing, which I wouldn't have dreamed, but if I had dreamed, it would have been with someone more exotic, unreachable, someone more a challenge. Not just the person closest to hand.

Harry's hands were on her. Every pore of my skin ached, seeing that.

When Harry hired her he said, "I can't believe how she's just moved in and taken over. She's very young to be so confident."

"She makes your work easier then?"

"You bet. It's only been a week and she knows where everything is and who to put off and who to get back to right away and she's not a pain in the ass about it, she doesn't have to keep coming to me with questions." He laughed. "In another couple of weeks I won't have to go in at all, she'll be taking care of everything. You have no idea how rare it is to find somebody you can depend on."

Well, I thought I had some idea.

"Of course," he said, "she's been in the company for a year so she understands how the operation works. But still, it's not often you find somebody who just does her job and does it right and isn't bugging you all the time."

When we were first introduced one day when I went to the office to meet Harry after work, there was nothing about her that made me notice her particularly. Nothing that said she was efficient or remarkable or anything at all. She was pretty enough, but not beautiful, but I hadn't expected her to be beautiful. When Harry spoke of her skills, I assumed she did not have beauty. He would have mentioned that.

The day we met, her blonde hair was pulled back and not glamorous, although later I sometimes saw her with it down, curling around her shoulders. The only make-up she wore that I could see was a slash of lipstick. She was wearing a white blouse tucked not very carefully into a tailored grey skirt, a grey suit jacket slung over the back of her chair. Proper office wear, I suppose, although not something I would have chosen. Too stark. Blue eyes, but set a little too far apart, and a nose just a shade too flat. Wide mouth, and a plump chin that would likely double some day, if she weren't careful.

If I close my eyes and concentrate, I can hear the sounds of my heartbeat and my pulse. I can almost hear the blood in the veins and arteries. There are shifting patterns of lights and shapes against my eyelids, and I can almost begin to feel how it all works, the internal intricacies. Could I trace the dangling, disconnected pieces?

Admirable, how the body goes on, performing its own routines, whatever is going on outside. It may speed or slow in a mild response, but basically it keeps functioning. Blood winds to the smallest places, food and drink are pulverized and acidized and moved, shifted, absorbed, the nerves send impulses, knowledge and memory leap in the brain, it all goes on. Hair and toenails grow and are clipped and then grow again.

I wish I could live as blindly and dumbly as the hair and toenails, I wish I could restore my ignorance. I would like to be a drop of blood, or a heartbeat.

When I called him at the office, she always said, "Oh hello, Mrs. Cormick, I'll just ring through and make sure he's not in a meeting." If he was on another line and I had to wait, she'd come back on and say, "He'll just be a minute. How are you? We haven't seen you for a while," and I could say to her, "I'm just fine, how are things going there?"

It didn't mean a thing, but that's just it: she was cheerful, friendly, and ordinary, and didn't mean a thing.

Really, I knew nothing about her except what Harry said: that she was quick and efficient and the best secretary he had ever had. Dear God, I expect that was true. I could even feel sorry for her. That she was in her middle twenties and worked at what must be really a dreary sort of job, you would think: typing, taking dictation and orders. "Does she have a boyfriend? Is she engaged?" I asked Harry. "No, she says she isn't interested in settling down." It was not a matter of settling down, as far as I could see. It was a matter of being safe and purposeful, not drifting.

Apparently she cared neither for her own safety nor for mine. Much less Harry's. I cannot imagine such a woman. Even Dottie Franklin is more comprehensible, her cruelty more human.

How did she feel, talking to me on the phone, seeing me occasionally in the office, seeing Harry hold my elbows and kiss my cheek? How did that feel to her? Did she not care when we went out of the office together, going to dinner, just the two of us? Did she know things, did he tell her things, that made it unimportant? How was she able to speak cheerfully and normally to me on the telephone? Was she feeling sorry for me? Laughing? I may, of course, be wrong, because I have been wrong about a number of things, but I didn't feel or hear pity or laughter in her voice. She must have been cruel, though. Only a cruel person could play with other people's lives, and if she was, as Harry said, not interested in permanence, she must have been just playing.

She may understand that even games have consequences. I wonder if she is a bit afraid to live now?

But if she was cruel, what was Harry? He came home every night (almost every night) to me. He touched my body and ate the meals I cooked and wore the shirts I washed and ironed and walked over the rugs I vacuumed and put on the suits I picked up from the cleaners, and all the time he knew.

Did he, with me, think of her?

He let me lie beside him in the dark and say "I love you," and he said it back, and all the time he knew.

Who can imagine so much cruelty? A Hitler of the spirit, my loving Harry.

I can't see what it was. I picture her and all the times I saw her and all the times we spoke, and I can't imagine at all what it was that let her skim so carelessly over me and through my life.

Was it just that she was convenient and young? Was it only years that made the difference?

Here I have not exercised for months. There's no possibility of watching my diet, I eat what I am given. I have no use for make-up, no one to impress or from whom to hide lines. There is no reason to wear scarves around my throat, or darker shades of stockings to make my legs look slimmer than they are. I don't need, in the late afternoons, to change my clothes for something more attractive. I do not even need to be sure that slacks and blouses match.

There is no reason to look into a mirror. Except to notice changes.

I am, perhaps, coming to look my age. I am sure I must look more than forty, and I may look forty-three. As I suspected, it happens quickly, when it happens.

I can't quite make out the whole effect. The woman who comes around each week to wash and set my hair (and all the others', too) twists it back with flying hands until it's all pinned down and set there. "Very chic and smart it makes you look, dear," she tells me, standing back and looking at her work. I don't know. I see only dark and greying hairs pulled back.

I can see, though, that for all the stuffy food and lack of exercise, there does appear to be some drawing in of skin around the bones. The skin itself is almost translucent, a kind of glowing paleness that might nearly shine in the dark, one would think. There is a caving in of sorts. I find my clothes hang oddly, loosely; like my mother stumping around in her oversized boots, going out to hang the wash. My eyes, blue in the midst of brownish-grey skin around them, peer. And in return, I sometimes notice people, visitors, staring at me.

What are they looking at? What do they see? Something odd, off balance? Some mark of what I did?

I try to count my grey hairs to see if there are more, but I keep losing track. It's so frustrating, not to be able to do what should be such a simple thing.

Sometimes I do get angry, having to start again and again.

27

VERY SOON NOW, it's going to be spring. This will be the third season since the event, which seems to have moved back so far in time, and also to be rolling up ahead again. I am a different person. Like being born in a late July night. An ugly birth that is, my life from his, a terrible thing. I should feel guilt and grief. I feel a little badly that I can't feel those things. The newborn Edna seems somewhat deformed.

It is difficult to remember that other one. Who spent years thoughtlessly and randomly, for all their order. At the time, it wasn't so hard. It's seeing that's hard, not blindness. I had my books and magazines and work and Harry, and the music, and it gets easier, not harder, to take for granted and not think. You don't even notice.

Now here I am, reduced to me, this pen, and this notebook, which appears to be less but may be more. And a great problem approaches: that this place, which looked so large and limitless when I began, is now becoming tight and dull. I don't quite know where to go from here.

I have examined enamel in sinks, complexions of people, myself minutely. I have kept up with imperfections. I have written precisely, if too often off the track. My notebooks are stacked neatly in the drawers of my half of the bureau. I have considered leaves and roses and the doctor. I have taken apart a pen to see how it works. I have peered until new lines have sprung up around my eyes. I have noted paint chipped from the corridors and the black numbers on the doorway to this room. I have kept my posture straight, my ankles neatly crossed. I have walked and run and noted the muscles pulling in each move. I have eaten hundreds of meals, I have eaten every kind of meal they have here, and the textures, colours, the variations are so minute now that despite myself I begin to wonder.

Was there a missed spot, an unremarked detail? Or something else entirely: Harry and me. Or only me.

I know there are tinier details, much smaller things to notice. But with human eyes, there is a point beyond which it is impossible to see. Human eyes do not reach the limits of vision. There are microscopic bits; and maybe even further bits, beyond the powers of a microscope.

The bedspread — just one thing. It is white and rough. But when I look more closely, I can see the fibres twisting all together, and from the fibres still smaller strands of thread, and I expect if I had stronger eyes I would see them furring out individually as well, and eventually down to the very atoms, and then the nucleus itself of each of them. Then to draw back a little and see that although the bedspread is white, there is variety, shading, some fibres not as pure as others, some more worn, a shifting of whiteness. So that not even a bedspread is allowed to be what it appears at first and easy glance.

Before, I might wander my perfect home admiring light catching on a gleaming table, flat tugged-neat bedspreads, pure windows. I was enchanted by flawless glass, thought that to see through such panes was undistorted vision.

What would I see now? Now that I have learned to look more closely?

The trouble here, right now, is just how far my vision can extend. I would not, before, have rewashed a just-washed dish, or revacuumed a just-vacuumed carpet merely to be filling hands and time. And now I cannot re-observe and re-describe something already impaled by this pen in this notebook. There is only one time I can hear an old woman down the hall calling out "Help me, help me," again and again, and have it new. I investigate, go to see the body behind the calling, and am surprised at how tiny and frail it is to have such force in the voice. I write, today a small woman called all day for help. Her voice is loud and desperate and has a scratching sound in the throat. All she says is "Help me, help me." A nurse has gone to her at least three times, but when she leaves, the woman begins to call again, "Help me, help me." I don't know what kind of pain she has.

I sit writing in this chair; I walk and watch and what I write is a constantly diminishing possibility.

Before, when everything that could be done was done, I took a bath, changed my clothes, and changed directions for the evenings with Harry. But also I did wander, I did look for some perfection, a confirmation in the polished, dusted pieces of my home. I also had moments of blankness when it seemed nothing would ever be completed. But I knew Harry would be coming home, some time.

It is a shock when something absolute does happen.

I have harvested details like a crop and stored them here. There can't be many left, and what shall I do?

The trees and snow are changing as spring comes, the snow diminishing and dirtying, a lightening in the air visible even through the glass. More a smell than something to see. Rough bark and soon, sweet grass. Flowers. Outside, there would be a thousand things to touch, examine, and describe minutely. Outside, it might take years to exhaust the possibilities.

Still, would it not end here again, with more notebooks and a dwindling field of vision?

I watch the doctor as I sit across the desk from him in his office. His walls are blue and so is the chair I sit in. His desk is oak, I think. On it there is a picture of his family: a blonde wife leaning over two small blonde children, all smiling up at the camera; at him, if he looks at them on his desk. Would he forget them if there were no picture, is that why he has it there?

He is watching me, patient as ever, stringing out his endless questions. "Tell me about Harry, Edna," he is asking, but without much hope; mere habit by now, I guess. "Tell me what he looked like." I write down his questions.

"Was he tall? Thin? Stout? Did he have a beard? Blue eyes? Brown? Dark hair, blond, bald? Tell me about Harry, Edna." He's asked all this before; but the words, as always, flow meticulously across the lines of my notebook.

Could I ask him to let me go outside? Because I have surely learned at least to investigate alternatives before something happens. One should have all the facts one can get. I do not learn quickly, but it seems that I can learn.

It's hard, though, to ask. Changes this man with whom I've spent so many hours. He will become, the moment I put the question, a mere man, a doctor with authority, no longer someone against whose collarbones I would sometimes like to rest my head. The figure will be transformed, Edna the magician, altering substances with words. But an improvement over knives.

I take a deep, brave breath. "Could I go outside?"

He's jolted, I see his body jerk just a little to hear me speaking. I see him hoping and interested once more.

"Did you want to go outside?" and his voice is now alive, expectant.

"If I could." It is important not to waste words. They seize on words and try to turn them around, spare words are their weapons here.

"What would you do out there if you could? What is it out there you want?" He, now, he uses too many words, throws them around too easily, plays with them. The advantage is with me and my tighter, tinier weapons.

"I'd see what's there."

He's puzzled, it seems. "You mean you just want to go out and look around? Or are you saying you want out of here entirely. Did you want to go home, Edna?"

He is not so clever. He doesn't see so well. I was right, he was more interesting and important before I spoke.

"Outside."

He sits back in his chair, steepling his fingers beneath

his chin, looking at me. He's pleased, I see. He thinks he has me some place where he wants me.

Is that true? Or do I see everything out of kilter and off-balance now?

"Well, Edna, I'd like to be able to tell you that would be fine. I understand of course that you'd be wanting to get outside, especially now with spring almost here. The trouble is, I can't really give you that permission because I don't believe you're ready yet."

Does he not think I see well enough? How would he possibly know all the things I can see now?

"Ready?"

Now he's leaning forward, hands clasped together on his desk, intent on me; even a doctor, who must make so many hopeless attempts, is hopeful. But I am not here for his hopes. I'm just trying to find out what to do.

"You see, you haven't been well, Edna. That's why you're here, why the courts sent you here. Do you remember the courts and what the judge said?" I do not answer, and write the question down.

"Do you understand you haven't been well? Do you know what happened? Can you tell me what happened?"

He tries to go too far too fast. My eyes are down again, and I am writing. I will not look at him again. I can be silent and I can wait. He has no idea how much practice I have, how many years I perfected those skills, being silent and waiting.

"When you're well, of course you'll be able to go outside. And when you're really well, there's always a chance you'll be able to leave here altogether. We can work together on that, Edna. If you want to go outside, we can start to work on it. You can, if you let us help you to get well again."

I had a warm vision of him, and it turns out he, like Harry, is both ordinary and no match for me.

If I don't look at him, he must know it's finished. But no, he is stupid and still hopeful. "We could start right now. You could start by showing me what you keep writing all the time. Would you show me your notebooks now, Edna?"

More and more questions, that's what I'm writing at the moment.

"Well, Edna," he says finally, and sighs, "we'll talk about it again tomorrow. We'll find a way to get you outside, if you'll help. It's a shame to miss the fresh air and the flowers."

Like Harry, he is sly. But he is not my husband, and my purposes have altered.

At least I've found out what I needed to know: that I can't go outside. So my choices are clear. I can pursue the smallest of the bedspread fibres, peering my way to blindness, my handwriting getting tinier and tinier, like the details; or I can face the moment and the white and yellow daisy clock. Tunnelling in or spiralling out.

I call it a choice; and yet like many other things, I can see it isn't.

What difference does it make? I am still Edna sitting in this chair.

But you can sit and sit and still be a different person, sitting.

I am only Edna, all by myself, and not important or strong. That must be something, although I can't say what.

It is reasonable that fear should be slipping away. There's nothing more to be lost, and nothing terrible, nothing left that deserves terror. I have done my worst.

And yet I miss fear, mourn it, try to keep a grip on what remains of it. It has protected me for so long, and from so many things. I get lonelier and lonelier as it escapes. A more constant companion than Harry, my fear has been, and I am losing it, too.

It's that white and yellow daisy clock. It dances on the bedspread and obstructs the other vision. There seems to be no getting around it.

28

LIES AND LIES AND LIES.

Who was she to be more than me?

Oh, I have tried not to see precisely. But there it is, the sweating bodies rolling and touching.

And then he could come home to me, join me in our bed and lie.

Did they talk about me? About us? If he could go into her bed and her body, what else? What did he keep from me to give to her? Bodies slithering together, words and touches.

He was wrong. He did wrong. If we may have said lies to each other, or left truths unsaid, they were our lies and truths. He should not have taken them outside to someone else.

It didn't occur to me that he might do that. And that's trust, isn't it? It's the same thing, isn't it?

But he did it; he betrayed belief.

What if I had said to him calmly, "I know. I know all about it." What might have happened? I think he would have said, "I'm sorry, forgive me, it will never happen again, I'm sorry, forgive me." And no doubt I would have. What else would there have been to do and go on living? I would have bitten and chewed and swallowed the rage and we would have gone on. The pain would all have been inside me, instead of inside him. But we would not have looked at each other again. We would have skirted and been polite, and I would have been alone. Either way, I end up alone.

I could stop it all now. There must be so many ways here: poisons and hanging and razors in the night. Pills, perhaps. They are careful, but no care is enough. I know that better than they ever can.

I didn't mean to be entirely alone; and I never intended for people to stare.

Harry promised I might live to eighty? Oh, surely not.

Could I not make it end right now? Would that be cowardice or courage? Where there's a will there's a way. My mother used to say that. She would not have blundered about like this, she would say, "Really, Edna, you'll have to learn how to work these things out. You have to do some things for yourself. You have to make your own decisions." But when did I pay attention to my mother, except as a poor example?

Tough woman, though. I wonder if she was lonely? I wonder if she is lonely now.

Stella might say, "Just take a run at it from a new direction. If it didn't work, leave it behind you."

It hurts to move though. I might like to dance, but it hurts to move.

Oh Harry, why aren't you here to tell me things I need so badly to be told?

Poor Harry, to have been loved with such a grip. To have carried my small weight upon his back for so many years. No wonder he began to stoop.

Maybe he would have preferred it if he hadn't been able to find a clean shirt, or if all his meals hadn't been as pretty as a painting, a still life. Two white vegetables in the same meal might have suited him just fine. He might not have cared a bit. He was maybe tired.

It's even possible he did not find by chance a hole in the great wall I built so carefully around us, our shining wall, but instead deliberately made one, tunnelling through with his long, slender, talented fingers.

I built so carefully and for so long. The two of us, we both made something, it wasn't only me. And it can all be destroyed in a phone call, a sentence, a moment.

Or, on his part a whim, a desire, a selfishness, a lie.

At least the pain is cleaner here than there.

But it's much colder here. I am so cold.

I used to be warm, so well-covered and safe. I thought all that padding, all the layers of soft warmth behind the wall, would keep me safe.

Maybe I should have left some part of me exposed. Because I failed to hear voices or see signs. I missed so many things.

Real passion — how would that have been? What would it have been like to really feel Harry's skin, and my own, instead of turning it into something tougher, harder — protection? How would it have felt if there had been nothing between us? What if I had understood those hands, the body, all the words he spoke, were someone else, another person, a life?

I took the face he gave me and transformed it into something else.

I wiped myself off like a child at the blackboard and then both of us must have gone about writing on it something wrong.

Is it something like being in a convent? To be a nun, with rules and times and faith, no questions? Is God like Harry? When they spend their lives for God, in the end do they go before Him thinking they're paid up, and does He turn away? Does He say, "That wasn't what I wanted at all, you made a mistake"? What a thing, to go for judgment and love, for reward at last for all the work and sacrifices, and have Him reject the gift. And then turn around and accept a sinner who has never made a payment. Would there be anger in the saintly hearts? Would they reach for knives and kill God?

Where is the gratitude? Who pays? Who rewards those nuns if they go before God and He says it wasn't necessary?

Maybe He says, "But you shouldn't have believed, that was a mistake. Faith made it too easy for you, it's not supposed to be so simple. You took too much for granted, you assumed all I wanted was for you to follow rules."

Would He offer second chances? Might He say, "Now lose your faith and see what happens, there's your test. Try again and see what you can do without it."

Is it possible to hope if there is no faith?

Somebody should know, somebody ought to be able to tell me what I was supposed to do, what the real rules were. It isn't fair that no one told me. Everyone kept these secrets from me, and they must have known. It would be like seeing somebody starting off across the country thinking they were on a main highway and not telling them they would wind up on a dirt track ending nowhere.

This mistake, this crucial misperception — a deformity, like being born with two heads or one arm. I am missing something that should be there.

Maybe God would say, "If I take away your rules, if it's not simple any more, you'll find out what you can do yourself. You have to muddle around until you find out what your own rules are."

What would my own rules have been?

I can't imagine. It doesn't seem to have been my life at all; although it must have seemed like my life at the time.

Where did I learn what I did? My mother used to say, with her usual impatience, "For goodness' sake, stand on your own two feet, Edna," so obviously not from her. My father, poor man, gave no advice. I did not want what they were, but the opposite. A queer backwardness of rules.

What would my own rules have been? If I were free, what would I be?

Oh, I might dance and dance, my body might tell tales, it might move like water. I might fling my arms wide and lift my body, spring up from my legs and my hair would fly around my face. I would shout and laugh out loud, I would feel blood pouring through my body, and I would stretch my earthbound fingers up as high as they could go.

In my life I might have shouted and laughed out loud and cried my tears. I might have said certain things to Harry, or thrown a glass at him. At parties I might have smiled and joked and flirted. I might have been all teeth and glitter.

Now I might carry placards up and down in front of the offices of magazines and shout out how they lie. That if they say that if one does this one gets that, it's only what is easy, not what is true. I might warn others not to believe truths handed out on pages.

I might rage out loud.

I am a forty-three-year-old woman who has not danced or often laughed out loud. I am a forty-three-year-old woman who has drudged like a nun for salvation. My glitter has been a smile or a pat on the shoulder or being held in the night. My joy has been gleaming glasses and waking to the sound of a snore.

My reaching up has been a leaning down to vacuum or pack trash. My flinging arms have only touched Harry, and barely myself.

Who taught me, and when? Who said, "Be still, Edna, don't move, don't make a sound and you'll be safe"?

It wasn't in me to be a dancing girl; I did not have the gift, and I could not help what I was.

Could I help what I did? Harry pointed out so long ago that being and doing might be different things.

Now I am tiny here in this tiny room, whirling in diminishing circles to the absolute moment, the world grows smaller and smaller and my life is a pinpoint of a moment. All my thoughts within twelve hours and my life within an instant.

The notebooks have filled the bottom bureau drawer and have begun to make their way into the middle one. My underwear and toiletries are crammed into small spaces now, making room.

All the blue covers, grey lines, pink margins, and even holes, filled with all the meticulous writing. All the vital letters of my life. And the paper no longer binds the wounds. Blood seeps between the pages, and oozes out the covers.

29

A LIFETIME OF THOUGHTS IN THOSE TWELVE HOURS. All of it was clear, if not comprehensible.

"I'm sorry, Edna," said the woman's voice. "But I thought you ought to know." Explaining everything. "They were kissing. What other explanation could there be?"

My glossy living room. The couch on which I was sitting, the couch on which Harry and I sat together. Where I held his hands and traced his fingers and believed they could do anything. (And they could.)

The chair from which I'd sometimes watched him, still amazed that he was in this room and that I was in this room with him.

All the other rooms now out of sight, my perfect home; except that the vacuum cleaner was still sprawled upstairs waiting, work unfinished. That nagged a little. But not right now. To go back upstairs and flick the switch, restart the motor, look beneath the beds for dust, push carefully into corners, not right now.

Downstairs was finished. After all the years, it was truly finished, the cleanness frozen. No more holding the toaster over the garbage, dislodging crumbs, and wiping the counter beneath it. Or drawing a cloth across the windowsills, or picking up a cushion to punch it fresh. No more dirty dishes or smudged windows or bits of dust in the corners of shelves. It had not seemed possible to ever finish; but here it was, done now.

The new gold-flecked white wallpaper had my full attention.

The house was airless. Once, Harry shouted at me because we were out of lemonade. He was angry because it was so hot, a heavy, stifling day, and maybe for other reasons, too. He went out and bought an air conditioner. We did not quarrel again because of heat, but the windows had to be kept shut. It disconnected the house from the world, and one might be startled, struck, by walking out the door into a different atmosphere. This was not a different atmosphere, however, but no atmosphere at all; the air sucked out leaving me holding my breath.

Pain, yes, of course. Odd, though: I could tell the pain was there, but could not quite feel it. It left a hole instead of a presence of pain. Quite a different sort of pain from skinning a knee in a fall, or from cutting a finger on paper. A gap of pain. Shocks like lightning behind the eyes, and weightlessness, a whipping away of solidity like a tablecloth from beneath a setting of dishes, so that I might rise and float into the air, away, or crash.

Time like a stop watch: the action halted at the finish. Forty-three years. So busy, time filled or put in, time in which to do things or time by which to have things done, time for home-comings and different little tasks and leavings, time for coffee or for waking up, time passing, time running out, time gone.

Time suspended like the air. Only the gold-flecked white wallpaper timeless and airless to hold onto. If I fixed on it firmly, I might not vanish.

No need to go through it year by year, moment by moment, like a photograph, it could be taken in at a glance. But cruel, a staring into the sun, a blazing on the eyeballs, after keeping the head down for so long. The eyes, unprotected and naked, were easily scorched.

Two phone calls in a day. The second the familiar trusted voice, but tinny, like a poor recording, down the line. No need to move, the arm reaches out on its own accord, no need for the eyes to wander, the arm lifts, flexes, and the ears hear the warm voice that is no part of this. Like those queer moments of seeing from the corner the two of us in bed; or stories I have read of people dying, a watching part moving away, shifting off, looking back with distant disinterest at the heavy shell of body now unrelated. His voice wholly a mystery now, if not the words.

"I'm sorry, Edna," he is saying from so far away, another life, some other level altogether. "But I'll make it home at some point."

"Yes."

"Is something wrong? You sound funny."

"No."

Did he use the pause to tell himself it was all right to be free? That there was no need to pay attention? He must have needed many times to reassure himself, or how could he have kept on with what he did?

"Okay then, if you're sure. I'm sorry. Tomorrow I'll definitely make it home for dinner. Listen, you're sure everything's all right?"

"Yes."

Even to me, my voice sounded odd; as if it were coming from outside, no internal resonances.

"I'll be as early as I can. It's this damned job."

"Yes."

The remote muscles of the arm on their own again, replacing the receiver without a fumble, no need to look. So many things can be done without a glance, it seems; so what need is there for twenty-odd years of vigilance?

The important thing to watch was the gold flecks on that white wallpaper, the light changing on it, afternoon moving into evening, sun from a new direction and fading. If the light went out entirely, there would be no seeing those gold flecks; and if I could not see them I would lose my balance, topple, slide, dissolve. There would be no holding me.

In the grey dimness of late evening, my arm reached out again, thumb moving for the switch on the table lamp and finding it, the light flaring on. It was possible, if still dim, to see the golden flecks; the main outpouring of the light on me now, but enough reflecting across the room to where I needed it.

There was a certain warmth, I could feel, from the light.

I wanted to keep very still, apart from that necessary move. I needed to be careful, because I was precious and fragile like a piece of transparent china, and could easily be tilted out of place and broken.

Sounds changed like the light. They, too, were far away and outside, like my voice. There were bird songs, until it got very dark, and cars on the street. Sedate here in this proper neighbourhood, no peeling rubber or screeching brakes. Lights flashing, reflected from cars or the houses near by. In those other houses people moved from room to room, came home, went to the bathroom, watched television, or trudged upstairs to bed. Even with the windows closed, I could smell steaks barbecuing in the early evening. All those people doing all those familiar things. Things I might have been doing yesterday. Everything now so changed that each move they might be making, each move I had once made, just yesterday, all of it so ordinary, normal, was now unimaginably exotic. A different world I was in now, and I could see only the reflections of their lights.

Not lonely; remote. This was so far away that to have been lonely would not have been so distant. It would have been a connection of some sort.

All of it gone as if I read or watched it.

I learned to walk, standing only to my mother's thighs, looking up, up at the lines beneath her chin, the hard setting of the jaw, a throbbing in the neck; a smell about her of clean laundry and hard work. And my father's sad eyes, and their voices over and across me. Tiny Stella, bland baby eyes closed: my mother and father united once, staring down at her. I was beside them, looking up at them. Had they stood over me that way, together and wondering?

Hair and make-up and menstrual blood. Dances and music and easy feet and longings. The passion of mirrors and pillows. Hearing Harry's voice for the first time, and later lying down beside him, surveying his long and narrow body as if he were sunshine. This was no mirror and no fantasy, but completion, purpose, end.

There were poets and dark-skinned men; but this was in my apartment and in my bed and his hands blotted longings as if they were tears, and the cloth of his body wiped mine clean, and soothed it.

I could not have done less in return. He contained me: all the people in our life, all the magazines and quizzes and recipes, the scrubbed floors and shining dishes and matching dinners, all the wine and laundry and supermarket shelves, all the vacuumed rugs — in one slender body, all of this.

Gone like the air, astonishing blow.

Darkness all around, except for the brightness on me, reflecting on the wall. Lights outside flicked off, and there were few headlights to sweep the walls any more. Only the lamp and the dancing, glittering, golden specks.

I might be motionless forever. I might never move a muscle. I might sit and breathe and die. I could be still, I had often been still, although not like this, not frozen. But this was my whole life here, breathing in and out until it stopped, watching the golden flecks.

I might know everything now. I might see clearly. There were forty-three years here, not hard to know all about them. Except for why, of course.

I saw through myself like glass; but could no longer see Harry at all.

There was a crackling on the gravel driveway he kept saying should be asphalted; but never did. Rare for him, procrastination, except he said he thought gravel might be less slippery in the winter. The rumbling of the garage door going up, slamming car door, garage door down. Such familiar sounds. Sounds that on other days I had leapt up for, a springing in the stomach. Tonight there was no one in the hallway taking a last glance into the mirror, checking hair. Some time earlier I must have taken my last glance and not recognized it.

The key was quiet in the lock. Oh, I had the senses of bats to hear so sharply through doors and walls.

The front door swung open and there were footsteps, and it clicked shut. Solid door, closing with a clunk, always safe behind such a door, no intruders, no one seeing in.

A quiet padding of steps upstairs. Above me I could hear him like a thief. Water ran and toilet flushed. Doors opened and shut, feet moved more quickly. A voice, the friendly ordinary voice but at a slightly different pitch, was calling, but so far away. Feet moving faster, and without efforts to be quiet, not to disturb. Running down the stairs and the voice louder. It called my name with a question mark, but I was all silence inside.

He was moving around and then he was in the living room and the footsteps stopped abruptly. I could feel the foreign presence. I was safe though, if I did not look and if I kept quite still.

He would have been wise to go away, but he wouldn't have known that, of course.

Two long legs in front of me — could I have leaned forward and caught her scent? I could see past them to the wall and held to that.

But the two long legs bent and lowered, a trunk appeared, chest, neck, face, hands so close, on my knees, face earnest and concerned, and altogether it blocked the view. I peered and peered, but couldn't see through that face, so handsome and fearful. The golden flecks danced for a moment in his face, but faded. Impossible to hold them. The familiar face unfamiliar, strange and bewildered, mouth moving in a babble.

I could hear my thoughts. I thought, "It does not all end here in this face. That is wrong, a mistake."

Without a place to look, the loss of balance, toppling, sliding dissolution, began.

The muscles trembled and were tender, the legs were weak, standing after so long a time. How rigidly they must have held themselves for all those hours. But some core in there to hold them up, to move them, a foot shifting with the impulse of this leg and then the other, this is what walking comes down to, again and again. The voice was loud, shouting and why, I was not deaf? I just wasn't listening.

What was it he wanted so badly? Not me, and too late for that anyway. I could feel his hands and fingers, well-known admired hands and fingers, clutching at my arm, my shoulder, trying to restrain. Not to hurt, not to be unfriendly, just a force to hold me back.

But my, I was strong. He could not begin to match me now. I could brush him off like a fly.

Although my skin could still feel his fingers when they were gone, dents and wounds like burn marks, cigarettes stubbed out in the pores.

My feet were moving to the kitchen, the light and yellow kitchen. The light was on — he must have looked for me here already. Here was the table where recipe books were read, cigarettes smoked, coffees drunk, meals planned, meals eaten, wine uncorked, and glasses raised. The smiles exchanged across the table hovered over it, the lying angels. All the lying moments in each kitchen tile and cupboard. Every thread of yellow curtains and each drop of yellow paint a lie. Each tap on the sink and each element on the stove, all the chairs and the two plants, each green leaf on both the plants a lie.

Dark outside the window above the sink. So many hours spent here staring out, while hands did other things: washed dishes here in this sink, and dried them. Cleaned vegetables and pared them, peelings from potatoes, carrots, onions, dribbling in. All the mouthfuls and forkfuls of food prepared here in this room. To fuel the lies.

False vitamins and phony colours. Beside the window, above the sink, a rack of wedding-present teak-handled sharp steel knives. Five: the smallest for paring, the largest for carving. The middle one sharp for tomatoes and other delicate things.

I am turning, and see him again. Now he is more than

frightened. Not concerned-frightened, but terrified, I see, and backing away. His hands are reaching out towards me and the sounds are much louder and higher-pitched, shouting on a different level. The hands do not reach for me, but against me. Something new here, the voice and the expression.

I am so strong. I have never been so strong before. I wonder why I didn't know I could be stronger than he was?

It does not go into him so far that it is necessary actually to touch him. The softness is pleasing and surprising, and I experiment with it again; several more times. It is a little like digging a trowel into soft earth in the spring to plant a flower. Once there is some hard impediment, like a root or a rock, but it's easy to twist around that, back into the softness.

It is the way I once thought making love would be: a soaring loss of consciousness, transcendence, and removal. I have gotten out of myself at last — so this was the way; and I am joined and free. This instant is wholly mine, and I am so free and light, tiny and light, a helium being.

The white daisy clock on the kitchen wall, with its yellow petal hands reaching from the yellow centre, it goes so slowly, slowly, in the silence. The moment is only a moment. His face and hands have vanished, and the moment disappears as well.

But now I know it is there; I have proved that it exists.

The silence rings and echoes and the hands of the clock are slow.

It is like resting my head on Harry's shoulder afterward.

Outside in the black, I hear voices, some shouting. The silence stops ringing. I find myself holding the tomato knife stained brighter than the fruit. Under the tap the stain washes off red and thick and glossy, catching onto fingers and fluttering away under the hard blast of water. I slide my fingers up and down the blade until the red is gone and the shining silver shows through again. The wooden handle, with the carved indentations for fingers to grip, is harder: the red does not come out of the grain so easily.

It is dried, and replaced where it ought to be. There are small stains and smudges in the ridges of my fingertips and my palms, and I wash my hands clean and wipe them on a towel.

I could move through this house blindfolded, or blind. I step back to the living room, the familiar room where the lamp still glows on the gold-flecked white wall. It is different now; the waiting is finished. I sit down to try to pick patterns from the swimming golden flecks.

Much better than cooking the perfect meal, or shining the perfect crystal. I have accomplished something here, I have found the moment.

30

IT IS STRANGE THAT NOW THAT HE IS NO LONGER WHOLE, I can see him, his bones and skin and hair adding up to something. A glinting Harry standing looking at me: I can see his pores as clearly as my own. He's a good-looking man, but not so very handsome. He was never intended to be a god.

I regret that he is dead, I'm sorry. But I can't seem to make the connection.

It was rage, not love, that gave the moment clarity and purity.

Poor man, poor stranger, poor Harry, whoever he was. I expect there was a time when he loved me, whatever that meant to him and whoever he thought I was. Poor me, poor stranger.

Some other Edna with some other life. Reincarnated here, with a magician's poof she appears, sitting in this chair between this wide window and this narrow bed.

Somewhere is a child Edna kissing pillow and mirror and man. But they are all gone; the mirror is shattered, the pillow shredded, the man torn.

If I can do anything, what shall I do?

What should I do, being free?

Put down the pen, perhaps. Set my feet up on the windowsill and cross my ankles; slide down in the chair a little; close my eyes and fold my hands.

I might let dust collect, lint gather, pins pile up in the carpet.

I would walk through the town I grew up in, peer in the windows of the house there and stare at the rooms and the lives, my silent parents watching television. I might touch my mother's shoulder, and kiss my father's cheek. I could look around and see if I could spot what frightened me. See if anything still frightens me.

I would write to my sister and invite her to join me, to come and look through the windows with me. I might hold her hand, or put my arm around her.

I might conjure up the running laughing boy behind me, and turn and look and see if the face was really the one missing from the mirror and the pillow. See if it was magic.

If I could see that face again, I might weep for it.

I would write a poem and see what words there might be for all this.

I haven't ever danced, and I would like to.

But I can dance now if I want. So I whirl around this small room, between the beds and dresser; I hum music to myself and lift my feet. Dancing alone, I can move my body as it wants. If I close my eyes, I am a dancer.

If I open my eyes, people are standing in the doorway watching, amazed. They think I'm crazy; and it doesn't matter a bit what they see. I find I am dancing with my eyes open now.

I can stretch and turn, kick myself into the air and land again, and if I step on my own toes or fall down, it doesn't hurt, it isn't dangerous.

I can whirl myself out of this room and down the hall; bend and reach and twist, leap or run. Elude the reaching hands. I could dance on my hands if I wanted.

It no longer hurts when I move.

I can dance myself silly. I can dance every moment of forty-three years. I can toddle-dance like a baby and glide like a grown-up. I can dance my lost babies and a house and Harry coming home. I can dance fear and pain. I can dance Harry himself, turn him into motion. He and his wounds flow through my veins and out my toes and fingertips.

I can dance tears and weep for Harry, and dry them again with the sweeping of a turn. It feels fine, dancing tears. I can feel his pain in my steps, his terror in my leaps. His bewilderment and confusion, and what he may have seen for twenty years, are in a glide. I can dance his eyes and his vision. I can feel his body finally in my own. I can tap along the blade into his body and weep some more, and once again dry the tears with a whirl.

I can dance his touches, of me and of her. I can dance lies. I can dance all the shining surfaces.

I feel muscles leaping, blood thundering, heart hammering. Like the dances, they want to leap from my body. Everything wants out to dance. Lost words too, all inside, clamouring like my lost children. I can dance and dance.

Not forever. The muscles and blood and heart are nearly forty-four years old and this freedom, the dancing, comes as a shock.

But while they can, I shall dance. I can dance all there is to be danced, as if there's no tomorrow.

There will be one, of course. A mystery, how it will feel. But it will feel something. I shall dance the freedom of tomorrow, eyes open, watching the people watching. I may sing, if I think of a song.

Whatever will become of me, this agile, dancing, fearless Edna who killed her husband and herself in another life? Another forty years, perhaps, to see; a medieval lifetime. A whole pure future in which to sketch a whole new Edna, the singer and the dancer, the free woman in the narrow corridor, alone in a small white bed.

Also of interest:

Joan Barfoot
Getting Over Edgar

**'As incisive and wry as Margaret Atwood . . .
Barfoot is plainly excellent'** *Spectator*

Seven weeks and three days before his death, Edgar walked
out on Gwen and their comfortable, long-standing marriage. To
aid his search for excitement, he had taken to driving a brand-
new cherry red convertible. But it is not adventure that sweeps
Edgar away when his car becomes stuck on a level crossing; it
is the 8.20 eastbound train.

In shock and distress, Gwen finds herself behaving in the most
inexplicable ways. Within weeks, she has sold almost all her
belongings, including the marital home. Then she sets off
across country alone, but not before she has committed an act
which will utterly transform her life . . .

Getting Over Edgar is the superb new novel from bestselling
author Joan Barfoot. It is a hilarious and deeply optimistic
exploration of human relationships, and the rich and various
possibilities of life.

**'Here is a novel that sneaks up and takes you by
surprise . . . clear-sighted and honest'** *Sunday Times*

'A strange and beautiful book' *She*

Fiction £6.99
ISBN 0 7043 4657 5

Joan Barfoot
Gaining Ground

Abra has left a husband, children and suburban security to live in an isolated cabin without mirrors, clocks or human contact. As time has passed, her senses have sharpened, her muscles hardened and she has achieved the inner peace and strength which had always eluded her before.

But when Kate, her daughter, tracks her down, Abra is forced to account for her actions and dramatically re-evaluate her life . . .

'One of those rare books which puts you in touch with yourself as deftly and as deeply as *The Bell Jar*' Nell Dunn

'Magnificent . . . An unusual and thought-provoking novel' *Manchester Evening News*

Fiction £6.99
ISBN 0 7043 3852 1